Author's Note:

This novel is a work of fiction. All of the main characters are fictitious and any resemblance to real persons is purely coincidental. Though settings, buildings, and businesses exist, liberties may have been taken as to their actual location and description. This story has no purpose other than to entertain the reader.

JOURNEY ON THE RAILS

By

Kileen Prather

I would like to thank the following for their invaluable assistance:

Bert Hermey@California Zephyr Railcar Charters,

Todd Powell @Vacations by Rail,

Nancy Becher for final editing,

Joe Chalok for his excellent advice with editing and other details.

And once again I dedicate this book to my

granddaughter, sons, and brothers.

May life bless all of you.

"One life and one alone
We have to live
Upon this little earth.
One life in which to learn so much…
To seek and find and prove our worth.
So many dreams there are to dream…
So many things to know and do.
So many rosy peaks to climb…
So many pathways to pursue."

Anonymous

Chapter 1

Chugga, chugga, choo, choo. The Zephyr gently rocked and swayed on the bumpy tracks as Phoebe looked out at the sea of corn fields flashing by. Sometimes the corn was broken up by fields of soybeans planted for crop rotation to put needed nutrients back into the soil. But mostly it was corn.

As the little towns out in the middle of Iowa passed by she wondered, besides agriculture, how these people made a living here among all this empty space. It would certainly not be an area she would consider residing in. But at the same time she knew that people here would hate living near a big city, as she did.

Twilight was rapidly descending. As she looked out the window of her rented Pullman car, she thought about how this journey had occurred. As she continued watching out the window she saw the reflection of a woman who was no longer a girl. When she turned off the last light the night sky, free of city lights, rapidly came into view

She often felt like a forty year old trapped in a sixty year old body. Phoebe took care of herself and exercised every day, but there were certain body parts that did not work as well as they used to with her knees being the best example.

Her friend, Riley, would always say "It is hell getting old", and as much as Phoebe did not want to admit it, she knew her friend was right. As she continued gazing out the window, she knew she could definitely lose twenty pounds. She now wore a size twelve. Although she did not look too bad, she longed for the days when a size ten fit perfectly.

With all that had happened to her in the past her therapist told her a few extra pounds would not hurt. He was proud of how far she had come, and this trip was the culmination of the last few years of counseling. Besides her health was good and she needed no pills for blood pressure or cholesterol issues.

"Just wait," Riley would say.

Continuing to stare out the train window, she saw an older woman with medium brown hair and glasses in the reflection. Although everyone said she did not look her age of sixty-two, she realized she was no longer the young woman she had once been.

Where had all the years gone? It had been eleven years ago. She had been fifty-one when Dan had finally been diagnosed, and it had been a long two and a half years of many inconclusive doctors' visits before the cause had been discovered.

When he was found to have early-onset Alzheimer's she was shocked. She remembered how she finally felt when she understood the reason for his inexplicable anger. She had studied about the disease as much as she could after the diagnosis. Then Dan died seven long years after his diagnosis. She began going on speaking engagements at Alzheimer's support groups to let others know what she had learned. She hoped to help them better understand the disease.

Through her research she learned that Alzheimer's is the most common form of dementia. At first memory loss is mild, but later people lose their ability to carry on a conversation or respond to their environment. In the beginning it is hard for the person to remember newly learned information.

As the disease advances through the brain it leads to more severe symptoms such as disorientation, mood and behavior changes and confusion about events, time, and place. Unfounded suspicions about family, friends or caregivers, along with difficulty speaking, swallowing and walking can follow.

She wanted others to know that when a spouse develops this disease, it is heartbreaking. The person you fell in love with and married is not the same anymore. In her case Dan soon needed her help with daily activities like bathing, shaving, and using the bathroom. As the years slowly went by his eyes became vacant, and he became unaware of his surroundings. The slightest thing would set him off. She remembered when he could not find his keys or cell phone. He would accuse her of taking them. And nothing she said would change his mind.

In the beginning if she mentioned anything to him about his behavior, he would lash out in anger, slam out the door and drive off. This was so painful, as well as scary, worrying that something might happen to him or others in his state of mind while he was driving.

And she was concerned whether he would find his way home. She was torn about calling the police. If they took his license away, how could she keep him from driving? As he worsened she knew he would forget about driving a car in time. Much as she hated that fact, she also looked forward to that happening.

She learned that up to five percent of those with the disease have early onset Alzheimer's. But how did that help her? What was even more frightening was that early-onset can run in families.

It is genetic but there are tests to determine if you have a higher risk of getting it. However, there is no single test to determine if one has the disease. That is why for over two years Dan's symptoms were mistakenly diagnosed as anxiety and depression due to his stressful job.

She talked about many things in her speeches. She would tell people how the disease does not progress any more rapidly than if you were to get it when you are older. There are medications that can help manage symptoms but none to halt the disease. Staying physically active and keeping connected with friends is very important no matter how old the person is. Dan was able to do that for about two years after his diagnosis.

Although he tried fighting the symptoms, once he was unable to articulate what was wrong, he became very frustrated. That put terrible stress on both of them. He became helpless, childlike and began shadowing her, as she was familiar to him even after he forgot her.

Then the violence began. His behavior got worse, and he would come up behind her and try to choke her. Once when she was bathing him, he punched her so hard her lip started bleeding. As she stood at the shower door, he seemed confused by her crying. However, he never unclenched his fist which continued to scare her. She knew he had not meant to do it, but he could have hurt her very badly.

Not long after he punched her, she decided it was time to place him in a residential home. However after a couple of months they asked her to remove him, as his violent behavior increased. So she took care of him at home with some big, burly male nursing assistants that she hired to help her. Since he did not sleep well at night she also hired an in-home caregiver to sit with him all night. It was the only way she could get any sleep. She thanked God every day that she had enough funds to cover these expenses.

For five years she felt such a sense of loneliness and emptiness as birthdays and holidays rolled around. Nothing they had shared was the same anymore. She loved him but it was such a difficult time because he was no longer Dan. It also saddened her that her two grandchildren would always remember their grandfather and his home as a place of sadness whenever they visited.

Her daughter, Laura, lived on the West Coast and was only able to visit three or four times a year. Laura called her every day and she treasured and looked forward to their talks. After her dad's diagnosis, Phoebe insisted Laura get tested. The relief they both felt when she was diagnosed negative was unbelievable.

That was why she went on speaking engagements. It

was because she felt so shell-shocked by what she had gone through with her husband. After he died she went to see a therapist, who thought it would be cathartic for her to talk about everything she had dealt with.

There is no cure, and so little is known about the causes of the disease, her prayer was that by getting the word out on a broader basis, hopefully more research and funding would happen. It is true that there is a greater chance of getting Alzheimer's since it is genetic. However anyone can be afflicted. Because of that she wondered about her grandchildren's future, if some breakthrough was not found for this terrible disease.

Perhaps her speaking out, would help others to deal with this problem. She hoped she could make them realize that they are not alone as the disease ravages their loved one and tears their lives apart. Sometimes knowing others are going through the same problems helps people to better deal with their own. As more and more baby boomers develop this disease, hopefully there will be more support for these people.

Extraordinary events don't define people's lives. Instead they detour them for better or worse. Dan getting sick was certainly a bad thing, but perhaps her speaking out to others made her life more worthwhile.

Her friends told her she needed to get a life! It had been four years since Dan died. But she kept thinking what if she fell in love with someone else, and he developed the disease. She just could not go through that again.

But as her therapist says, "You've come a long way, baby."

Chapter 2

Phoebe knew she should not dwell on what happened to Dan but in a way it was why she was now on the train. All their married life her husband had talked about a wish he had for when he retired. He wanted to rent a Pullman car, attached to an Amtrak train, and travel the Western United States.

He had belonged to a Wisconsin train club and since they lived outside of Chicago it was close enough for him to go on get-togethers with his train friends whenever he was able. Every chance he got he would take Phoebe to train museums, especially if there were restored Pullmans to be seen.

Dan had taken out a large insurance policy a few years after they had gotten married. He had made her promise if something happened before he retired, she would go on the journey without him. She had jokingly agreed to his request thinking nothing would happen to him.

So she had spent the last year researching her trip. Dan's friend, Todd, owned a Pullman car and it was a beauty. Todd loved renting out his Pullman, which came with a train attendant and cook, because it helped defray some of the costs of ownership.

It was quite expensive to rent a Pullman for the distance she was anticipating traveling. She definitely could not, and would not, do it on her own. The first person she talked into going with her was her friend, Riley.

Riley's husband had made a lot of money in the stock market before he died and she lived very comfortably off the investments and life insurance he had left behind. She thought it sounded like a fun adventure, and told Phoebe to count her in.

Riley was fifty-eight years old. She had short curly red hair, blue eyes and was a petite size 8. She had been married to Jake, the love of her life for over thirty years. She had been widowed for three years and was having a difficult time accepting her husband's death.

Jake traveled overseas for business quite a lot. Usually on long flights he got up and walked around every hour or two. But he had not been feeling well before his last trip and had spent all of his time sleeping in his seat both going and coming home.

He had no idea he had developed blood clots in his leg. By the time he got home he had chest pain, was coughing and having difficulty breathing. He did not realize the blood clots had flowed into his lungs. He only knew he felt terrible. Riley was worried about him and had driven him to the emergency room. As he exited the car at the hospital, he fell over dead.

The two women had encountered each other in the office of the therapist they both shared. When the doctor had gotten an emergency call they had met in the reception area of his office. As they were rebooking appointments, they started a conversation. Realizing they had a lot in common they started going out to lunch every week. It was not long before they became best friends.

Like Phoebe, Riley had no intention of ever marrying again. If it was perfect the first time, what were the chances that would happen again? Riley had a friend named Hugh. His wife, Hillary, had died. But he would never talk about her or what had happened. The two had met at a charity event and had become fast friends. Since neither of them was interested in having a serious relationship, they had an easy going friendship.

Hugh was what you would describe as tall, dark and handsome. He was six feet tall and Riley looked like a dwarf next to him. He had brown wavy hair with just a hint of grey and green eyes. He was sixty three years old and had retired at fifty-five having made his money in technology.

When Riley told Hugh about her upcoming train trip, he asked if they had room for anyone else. He thought it sounded like a wonderful adventure. He had a friend whom he knew would also be interested in going. Since they had grown up together and been friends all their lives, they would be willing to share a room if necessary.

Phoebe, knowing Riley would vouch for her friend, thought it sounded like a good addition. It would be quite expensive to do the trip she was planning, so the more people to split the cost the better. It would be fun having a few people along to share in the adventure.

Her Aunt Julia and Uncle Henry had also asked to come along. They were celebrating their sixty-second wedding anniversary and decided it would be a unique way to remember the occasion. Their only son had been killed in Viet Nam. As they had no immediate family to leave their money to they did not have to worry about how much the trip would cost. Since Phoebe knew they were comfortable but not wealthy she and Riley agreed they would count the couple as one when dividing up the cost.

There were five bedrooms in the Pullman, and Phoebe realized they would now be full. She and Riley would have their own rooms, her aunt and uncle would have another one. The two men would have to bunk together. The last room would be shared by the attendant and cook. Todd told her they usually shared a room unless there was a spare. Although they were not married, they had worked together on the Pullman for fourteen years and respected each other's privacy.

Phoebe wondered about the other man who was coming, but knew she would meet him soon enough.

Chapter 3

Phoebe and Riley were having lunch one afternoon at one of their favorite diners. Riley's friend had agreed to come meet Phoebe. As the women were discussing their itinerary, Hugh walked in with another man. He was not quite as tall as Hugh, and Phoebe guessed he was around 5'9"since he appeared a couple of inches taller than she was.

He had white hair and brown eyes just like she did. He seemed to be a very polite man, and you wanted to smile when you looked at him. Tony was Hugh's friend, and he was also sixty-three years old. Hugh had told Riley his friend had been divorced for twenty eight years.

He was very good looking, and must have gone through something traumatic to stay unattached so long Phoebe thought. He seemed a very agreeable man and thanked Phoebe profusely for letting him join them on their journey.

It was good having several people share the cost. At the same time Phoebe and Riley did not want anyone along who was bossy or unpleasant. That is why they wanted to meet the two men beforehand to make sure everyone was similar in temperament.

Riley had told Hugh that they needed to be compatible and that would be a condition of whether or not the women accepted them on the journey. Hugh said that was very smart of them instead of just taking anyone along. If someone got on your nerves, it could make for a very unpleasant time.

They still did not have all the details of the trip worked out, but they thought they would probably be gone about three weeks. Being in such close quarters it was important that everyone got along well. Riley had been out with Phoebe's aunt and uncle several times and knew they would be fun to have along.

Aunt Julia and Uncle Henry were very unassuming people and loved traveling. Her aunt had already given Phoebe some great ideas for the itinerary since they had been to most of the places they were going. She had also told Phoebe that whatever the group decided to do she and Henry would be fine with it.

"Riley and I were thinking of making a few stops along the way. What do you think?" Phoebe asked Hugh. "That's a great idea. I suppose we have to stop at the major cities since they have the capability to uncouple our car," Hugh said.

"Yes, that is what Todd said. We are being charged a flat fee for the use of the Pullman which includes our food and drinks and a per diem for the cost of the cook and attendant. We also have to pay Amtrak so much per mile, and there is a charge every time we couple or uncouple the car. You can understand why this is a costly venture."

Todd wants a specific amount the week before we leave.

This should completely cover our costs for the Pullman. He said if we did run over for some reason we can pay the balance when we return.

Riley then spoke up, "Phoebe has been in contact with the owner and has asked him many questions. She also contacted some friends of her husband who belonged to the same train club as he did. She has gotten some great advice. Obviously we do not know everything and since you are paying your equal share any input you have will be taken into account. We will be in close quarters for several weeks and need to be comfortable with each other."

"I want to thank you for letting my aunt and uncle be counted as one. They have traveled everywhere and have given me some good suggestions. Aunt Julia has already told me that the four of us should make all the decisions regarding our stops and sightseeing. They are good with whatever we decide."

"We know this was your idea and really appreciate being able to go with you. This is a really fun idea but we would never do something like this on our own. It will be nice to share the burden of the cost among all of us. We definitely appreciate you letting us have some input into the decision making," Tony said.

Hugh then spoke up, "Will you tell us about the Pullman. Have you seen it?"

"Yes I have," Phoebe replied. "It is really awesome."

"Phoebe and I drove up to southern Wisconsin where Todd keeps his car. So I also saw it, too. Phoebe is right It is awesome!"

"Tony and I looked up information about Pullmans online the other day. You may already know, but they have a very interesting history."

At that point Hugh spoke up. "Did you know George Pullman manufactured his railroad cars from the mid 19th century through the early decades of the 20th century when railroads were in their heyday? The workers who built the cars lived in a planned worker community (a 'company town') named Pullman. You can still visit this area today just south of downtown Chicago."

Tony then continued, "After spending a miserable night sleeping sitting up in a chair, Pullman began designing a railcar with sleeper berths. During the day the upper car was folded up and at night the two facing seats folded down to make a bunk. There were curtains for privacy. And although it was pretty spartan by today's standards, it was comfortable and private. Actually the concept is similar to what Amtrak provides now with their roomettes."

"Just like we are doing, Pullman operated his cars on most of the railroads by paying the companies to hook up his cars to their trains," Hugh added. "By 1862 Pullman began building luxury sleeping cars which had carpeting, draperies, upholstered chairs, libraries, card tables, and an unparalleled level of customer service."

Just like a tag team the two men were very excited talking about Pullman history. Phoebe and Riley had studied up on trains and had seen their Pullman, but they had not really delved into the history like the men had.

When it was Tony's turn to talk, he said, "These cars offered complete privacy. They were intimate, luxurious and a memorable way to travel. It was also a wonderful way to spend time alone with the people whom you cared about the most. The company used the trademark phrase 'Travel and Sleep in Safety and Comfort'. With over ninety-eight hundred cars by the 1920s people obviously believed the advertising."

As he continued Tony said, "When George Pullman died in 1897, Robert Todd Lincoln, Abraham Lincoln's son, took over as company president. After a strike in 1897 the court mandated the town be sold. The sale was completed in 1907. But the Pullman Company thrived all through the heyday of railroads. With more people driving cars and an interstate highway system coming to the fore in the 1950's, train travel began to diminish. In 1955 the company closed its factory in the Pullman neighborhood of Chicago, and an era came to an end. Today, as I told you previously, Pullman is a Chicago neighborhood and is listed on the National Register of Historic Places."

Chapter 4

The two women were very impressed with the history the men had just relayed to them.

"Wow. You really did your homework. Let me tell you about our car, and then Riley and I thought we could talk a little about our itinerary."

Riley was nodding as Phoebe continued, "Even though we will be coupled to an Amtrak train there is no way for people to walk from the Amtrak train into our car. The only way to get in is to go outside, walk over to our car and climb the stairs. That makes for complete privacy, because the attendant, the cook, or one of us will always be by the stairs at stops and will not allow anyone to board who does not belong. At night, when everyone is sleeping, the door will be locked."

As the men listened Phoebe resumed, "When you go up the stairs the first room you encounter is the kitchen. It is small, but space had been conserved quite well. There is a little stove, a refrigerator, microwave and even a small freezer. There are cupboards just like in a regular kitchen. According to Todd, the cook's name is Margaret. And since she has been working for him for fourteen years, I am sure she really knows her way around that little kitchen. She probably has her work area down to a science."

"Next are five bedrooms," Riley added. "And they appear very spacious compared to Amtrak's bedrooms."

"Maybe the men would like to know the Pullman's dimensions," added Phoebe. "The car is a little over 81' long, 14' tall and 10 & ½' wide."

Riley continued, "The first two bedrooms have twin beds. The first room is where the cook and attendant, Charles, will sleep. It is pretty small with a small dresser between the beds. The next room is bigger but it also has two twin beds. There is a larger dresser for clothes, and it has a table and chair. That is where you two will sleep. The next two rooms have a double bed with a dresser and two chairs. Finally the last bedroom is a little bigger with a Queen-size bed, a dresser, chair and vanity. I told Riley we would flip a coin to see who gets the bigger room."

"I told Phoebe the room was hers since this whole escapade was her idea. Her aunt and uncle and I will take the two double bedrooms. I hope you men are ok with the sleeping arrangements. Oh, and all the bedrooms have a small closet and a bathroom."

"It sounds great," said Hugh while Tony nodded in agreement.

Phoebe resumed, "Next comes a little bar area. I suppose it is there so that the help has someplace to put the food and drinks before and after serving us. Continuing on you climb up three stairs into the parlor. Although this car was built in the late 1940s, the owner had it restored in the rich

'Pullman green' colors of earlier days. Naturally you will notice the varnish on the walls. This was put on to protect the wood in the cars. There is black walnut woodwork, framed mirrors between the windows, French plush upholstery, polished brass fixtures, and deep pile carpeting. You almost feel like you are traveling in the Victorian era."

"It is a very impressive parlor," Riley added. "On the left side are two built in rounded couches with coffee tables. On the right side are some velvet brocade chairs with end tables. And there is a Victorian writing desk in a corner on the right in the back before the observation platform. When you first walk into the room to your left in the middle is another set of stairs to the dome car. Up there are two tables, actually booths, on each side with seating for four at each one. They can be used for eating, playing cards and games, or just watching the world whizzing by through the large observation windows. There are also built in cabinets on each side with counters to put the food and serving dishes on."

"Well, it certainly sounds incredible," the two men said at the same time.

"Do you realize we have been sitting here talking for almost two hours," Riley said. "Phoebe and I both have appointments in a half hour so we need to go. Besides this restaurant is going to close soon, because it is only open for lunch. I had no idea we would be talking so long, and we haven't even started on the itinerary yet. Today is Tuesday. Do you think we could meet for lunch on Thursday or Friday? It will probably take a couple of meetings to go over the itinerary, since we spent so much time just talking about the train today. And it would be nice to have a preliminary plan, so we could start researching actual attractions."

"That is a great idea, Riley. However both Tony and I have some obligations towards the end of the week."

The women did not know that Tony and Hugh volunteered at a shelter for children in foster care every Thursday and Friday afternoon.

"Why don't we have lunch next Monday? That will give the two of us time to research the routes and figure out what attractions look interesting. I believe your plan is to take the California Zephyr out to Oakland, California. Then we would take the Coast Starlight up through California and Oregon to Seattle, Washington. And finally the Empire Builder through the northern states back home. Is that correct?"

"Sort of Hugh. There are two things my aunt suggested which Riley and I thought were good ideas. First we will get off in Denver and rent a van and do a loop around the state to Grand Junction. There are quite a few historic trains in Colorado, and as long as we are there we should probably experience them. We would have our Pullman continue to Grand Junction without us, uncouple and wait for us to get there."

"That sounds like a great idea," Tony said.

"The other idea is to skip the Coast Starlight. It is a very nice train but there are only views of the coast between Los Angeles and San Francisco, and we would not get on until Oakland which is the San Francisco stop. Aunt Julia says the Oregon coast is awesome to drive. So we were thinking when we get off in Oakland our Pullman can continue on the Coast Starlight north without us. We can rent a van and drive through the Redwoods in California, the Oregon coast, stop in Portland and do the Columbia River Gorge, Mount St. Helens and finally Mt Rainier on our way to Seattle."

"That is another good idea, Phoebe," Hugh continued, "Not only will that save us on coupling and uncoupling fees, but your aunt is correct. I have been along the Oregon and California coasts and they are awesome. I noticed the train does not get near the coast in those areas and you will miss a lot by not driving. Perhaps we could have the Pullman stop in Portland, Oregon, so we can use it as a hotel when we are there."

"That is also a good idea. Sometimes we need to get hotels but since we need three rooms it would be good to use the Pullman whenever possible. So it is agreed," Riley said. "How about we meet next Monday at 12:30 p.m. at that new deli on 4th Avenue? Everyone I talked to said it is really good. And they use real meat instead of that processed stuff."

As they left the restaurant they waved good-bye, and the men went one way while the women went the other.

"You know, Riley, I get very good vibes from those men. They were never pushy, and we talked almost two hours agreeing on everything. I also liked that they did the research on the Pullman history. I have a feeling we will all be very compatible traveling companions. Considering how long we will be together that is important.

"I agree with you, Phoebe. I already know Hugh, and he is a very likeable man. And it seems Tony has a similar disposition."

Waving good-bye they got in their cars and went their separate ways. They still had about three months before their trip, and Phoebe was hoping to have a pretty good outline of their journey finished before they met again. She knew the week would fly by with all the research she wanted to do.

On the way home she stopped at her local AAA office. She did not want them to do a Trip Tik for her, but she did want maps and books for all the states they would be traveling through. Hugh had mentioned he would also stop by AAA for books and maps. Phoebe thought that was a great idea, because then they would have double sets in case something happened to one set.

Chapter 5

Even though it was Tuesday when they left each other the days flew by, and before they knew it Monday had arrived. It was a blustery, cold March day with overcast clouds that threatened rain when Phoebe and Riley drove into the deli parking lot at the same time.

Walking into the restaurant together they looked around for the men. Tony and Hugh were already at a table, and waved to the women when they spotted them coming through the door.

The two men stood up as they approached the table. Laughing Riley said, "If we are going to be friends and see a lot of each other, please do not bother to stand every time you see us coming. Although I have to admit, it was a very nice gesture. Have you ordered yet?"

"No, we were waiting for you. Hugh is starving so why don't we go up and place our orders. I guess they give us a number which we place on our table. Then they deliver the food."

After they ordered and returned to the table Hugh asked, "I am curious. Phoebe why did you decide you would do this trip in mid June?"

"Actually I asked Todd for his advice. He suggested mid June, because most families do not take their vacations that early. He also said that the 'Going To The Sun' road at Glacier National Park does not open until the end of June or the first part of July depending how much winter snow the park gets. Since being around a bunch of screaming excited vacation kids and their families does not do much for me, I decided he had a point. The weather can be very dicey at Glacier in September, so mid June seemed our best bet."

"I think you picked the perfect time," Tony said. "I have spent a lot of time in Colorado in July and August, and even though it is a dry heat the state can get quite hot even up in the mountains in those months. I do not mean to be rude, but can I ask if you have a problem being around children?"

"No, I love children. I have grandchildren of my own. What I don't like is being around families when parents have no control over their kids or let them do anything they want. One time I was at the falls in Yellowstone and a park ranger asked a parent to have their child step back on the other side of the fence. It seemed a child fell to his death every year by being on the unsafe side. The parent told the park ranger to mind his own business. Meanwhile other kids were yelling and screaming and pushing people out of their way. That it what I object to."

At that point their food arrived and the four of them concentrated on eating their salads and sandwiches. After they finished, Phoebe brought out two pads of paper. On one of them was an outline of the trip and the other was blank.

She began, "We talked about making Colorado our first stop. Tony, you mentioned previously you have spent a lot of time there. What are your thoughts on what we should do when we get there?"

"First of all there is no way we can experience all the wonderful trains in that state since there are so many. I know you have all studied up about trains and know that standard gauge, the distance between tracks, is 4'8 -1/2" wide. In Colorado most of the tracks are narrow gauge--3'6."

These smaller tracks were built because they needed to get the trains up into the mountains to the small out of the way mining towns. It was cheaper to build shorter width tracks especially around mountain curves. Since they had to retrieve the gold and silver, building smaller spurs seemed the logical way to accomplish this. Of course, that meant the train cars also needed to have a smaller width to run on those tracks."

Everyone nodded in agreement at what Tony said as he continued, "There are some wonderful examples of narrow gauge trains which I think are really highlights to be seen. If we are going to make a circle around the state as you suggested last week, Phoebe, I chose a few we should consider."

"I think you will like Tony's suggestions," Hugh joined in.

"Since it will be morning when we get off in Denver I think we should get the van and make our way immediately to Colorado Springs. It should only take us a little under one and a half hours to get there. We can drive though the Garden of the Gods on our way to Manitou Springs to catch the afternoon cog railway up Pike's Peak. Afternoon is probably the best time to go up that mountain, because the weather will be warmer that time of the day if it is not overcast. I am not promising anything, because when you are up over 14,000 feet any conditions can and may develop."

Tony continued, "We will stay overnight in Colorado Springs and continue to Canon City to catch the Royal Gorge train the next day. It is only two and a half hours after our train ride so we should easily get to Alamosa for our next overnight. The following day we will go to Antonito and ride the Cumbres & Toltec Scenic Railroad to Chama, New Mexico. We probably should drive to Durango for our overnight, and then do the Durango & Silverton train after that. Our time is limited, so if we take the early train and spend an hour for lunch in Silverton we should get to Grand Junction in time to catch our train at 4:00 p.m."

"I did not realize we would be going to New Mexico," Phoebe said.

"We just cross a little corner of the state on our way to Durango. We are actually pretty close to Santa Fe when we ride that train."

As he looked at them he added, "This timing is all contingent on just going one way on those last two trains. Otherwise it will take us longer and we will be in more hotels. I think we should call ahead to the train stations in Antonito and Durango. That way we can find someone to dead head with our van to the next stations which will help our plan to work. We can pay them a stipend and buy their lunch as well as a one way ticket on the train so they can get back home."

"That sounds like an excellent idea," Phoebe said. "But you are talking about spending at least four days in Colorado. At that rate this trip could turn into four weeks instead of three."

"Making all those stops along the way, as you are suggesting, is really going to add to the trip. But this is a once in a lifetime journey, and it would be a shame if we did not see everything we possibly could when we are traveling right past these sites. Besides, since we are splitting the costs and have the funds I do not think an extra week would be a problem. I think everyone has the time, correct?"

"You're right, Tony. It is a good thing we have three months to plan this itinerary. In May we should make a few hotel reservations where we think they are needed. We can always change them if necessary, but we will be going at the beginning of peak season. What with all of our specific stops we will need three hotel rooms each night as well as a van in each location. I will get a hold of Todd to see if we can have the Pullman longer. I think we will definitely need that extra week."

Riley then added, "I don't think we need to stop in Salt Lake, do we?"

They all shook their heads "no" at her question, since everyone had been there before. She then continued, "If we can fit it in, it would be nice to stay one day in Reno and go to see Lake Tahoe. Or, thinking out loud, we could spend two nights in that area and go to Yosemite. I have never been to that park and have heard it is wonderful."

"We can put that down as a tentative stop once we see how the rest of the itinerary falls in place," Phoebe said.

Then she added, "I know we could drive to San Francisco from Yosemite, but I think going back to Reno would be better. Todd told me the scenery from Reno through the Sierra Nevada Mountains with all the tunnels is really one of the Zephyr's highlights. I think we should ride our Pullman through that area."

"I agree," Hugh added. "Besides we will be in the van for several days, as we travel up the coasts of California and Oregon. I am looking forward to enjoying the Pullman as much as possible."

Looking at her notes Phoebe added, "The only stop I think we need to make on the Empire Builder is at Whitefish, Montana. I would definitely like to spend a couple of days in Glacier National Park before heading home."

"What an incredible trip!" Riley said. "I can hardly wait. But I can see where we have a lot of work to do in preparation." As she looked around the table, she glanced at her watch and said, "We have been at it almost three hours. Time certainly passes quickly, when we start working on this journey."

"It sure does," the two men said as they nodded in agreement.

"I am going to get a hold of Todd and see if we can get that extra week booked. I think we have Colorado sketched out enough for now. Riley, why don't you look into the Lake Tahoe and Yosemite regions and see what you think we should do there. You can also help me research from Portland to Seattle." Looking towards the men she added, "If it is okay with you, why don't you two men research San

Francisco and up the Pacific Coast since you seem to have some knowledge of that area. Tony, you can be in charge of Colorado. Is that agreeable with every one?"

"Dividing up our itinerary for research sounds like the fastest and most efficient way to proceed at this point," Tony agreed. "We can always fine tune our stops after we have a preliminary outline." Looking at the two women he continued, "I take it this means we have passed your guidelines and have been given the okay to go on the trip with you."

Looking at each other and laughing the women nodded "yes" at the men.

As soon as she got home, Phoebe called Todd and got the okay for the extra week. When she gave him a sketchy idea of what they wanted to do he also concurred with her and said they would definitely need the extra time; besides that would give more work and more income to his employees. Since he had nothing else booked during that time period, he was happy to give us the extra time."

Chapter 6

The four of them met every Monday for lunch to work on their itinerary. By May they decided they needed to meet twice a week and added Saturday afternoons. Everything was shaping up quite nicely. They had been able to add the Yosemite stop and were glad Riley had suggested it.

Phoebe had gotten in touch with Todd and had given him the dates of their stops. He needed to contact Amtrak with the dates they would be uncoupling and coupling. The travelers did not like having a strict time schedule, but Amtrak needed to know in advance. They had a few extra days so they built them into their schedule.

Deciding to leave Chicago on a Sunday put them at their hotels in Colorado during the week. They did not want to pay extra for hotels just because it was the weekend. They then made reservations for their hotels and the four train rides.

They also booked rooms at Yosemite in the Ahwahnee Hotel. It was expensive but the women were excited when they were able to book adjoining rooms with a shared balcony for themselves and Aunt Julia and Uncle Henry. There were only a few of these types of room so they were glad they had booked early.

After doing some research they decided to stay overnight in the Pullman in downtown Reno. Their van was reserved and they planned to do a lot of driving that day. They would visit Virginia City, Carson City (the capital), and drive part of Lake Tahoe before circling back on the interstate to Reno.

They would spend the night on the train and be ready for the coupling early the next morning. They would ride through the scenic Sierra Nevada mountain range to Sacramento, California's capital. It was only a couple of hours to Oakland, California and they decided the Pullman would continue to Oakland without them. It would be just as reasonable to stay in a hotel there than go to the bother and expense of uncoupling the Pullman.

There is a famous train museum in Sacramento in Old Town. They would spend one night in Sacramento and make the three hour drive to Yosemite the next day. That way they could drive through the park on their way to the Ahwahnee Hotel. The next morning they would take a tram tour that was available in the park before their five hour drive to Oakland. They would take a different route out of Yosemite, so they would see as much as possible of the park.

They decided to spend all their nights on the train in Oakland. San Francisco hotels were very expensive, and it was foolish not to make use of their Pullman when possible. They still had not decided on all their activities in the San Francisco area.

They were thinking of doing the city the first full day they were there. The next day they could drive down to Monterey and Carmel. On the third day they would go north to Muir Woods and explore a bit of the coast on Highway 1.

They knew there would be plenty of time on the train to firm up their itinerary in those areas. One of the tables in their dome car had already been reserved with a box for their maps, tour books and anything else research related. In that way one or more of them could study their plans without constantly trying to find maps or tour books. They also had a small satchel they planned to put on the table, so they could file away the materials of the regions they had already visited.

Todd had requested a list of dietary needs and requests so the cook could plan her meals. Actually no one was allergic to anything and had few dislikes, so that had been easy to do. Except for an occasional after dinner drink they had only requested wine be available. None of them were big alcohol drinkers, so that would also keep the cost down.

The only other big issue was their wardrobes. There was not much room for lots of clothes. Because of the different climates they were traveling to, they needed both winter and summer outfits. They each decided to take two suitcases. One would contain heavier clothes, and the other would have lighter clothes. As on a cruise ship their two suitcases would fit under their beds which would conserve space. Then they would all use one of their suitcases when they were traveling in the vans.

Leaving Oakland they would drive on Highway 101 which goes inland in that locale through the Napa Valley. By the time they got to northern California near the redwoods the highway would then follow the coast all the way north through Oregon.

Todd already told them the cook would do their dirty laundry when the Pullman was stopped at a station while they were out exploring. They would all be given laundry bags with their names on them, so their clothes would not get mixed up with the others. All they had to do was put their laundry bags on their beds at the stops and she would take care of getting everything clean.

They all decided they needed two sweatshirts/sweaters, two pairs of jeans, and a lined jacket with a hood that would protect them if it rained or was cold. Whatever else they wanted to take was up to them, although the men suggested bathing suits for hotel pool and hot tubs.

The Pullman also had WiFi which would come in handy for making new reservations and keeping in touch with friends and family. A TV/DVD player with Netflix had been mounted on the parlor wall, opposite the desk, in case they got bored. Phoebe and Riley both thought they would not be using the television much. Todd had probably installed it for parents with kids.

At last the end of the first week in June arrived. None of them could believe how fast the three months had gone by. It was Saturday afternoon, and they were leaving a week from Sunday. They decided they did not need to meet on the following Monday

They settled on one final meeting on Friday night. They would have dinner together, and Phoebe's aunt and uncle would also be invited. That way any last minute issues could be dealt with quickly.

Before they knew it they were all sitting around a table for six in a local steakhouse. Phoebe's aunt and uncle lived two hours from her, so they had driven to her place that afternoon. They planned to stay with her and leave their car at her house. Riley was being dropped off at Phoebe's house on Sunday morning. They had rented a limo to take the four of them down to Chicago's Union Station by noon where they would meet up with the men.

The train departed at 2:00 p.m. and they would wait in the first class lounge until departure time. Phoebe could almost hear the conductor saying, "All Aboard."

Chapter 7

The limo dropped them off on a corner at Chicago's Union Station. They found a Red Cap who loaded their suitcases onto a cart. They walked down a long ramp and entered into the Great Hall.

Normally the Red Cap would take them to the counter to check their luggage, but they tipped him extra to take the bags to their Pullman when the train pulled into the station. Because of that he went on with the cart to store the bags until it was time to deliver them to the train.

Riley and Phoebe had gone down to check out Union Station one rainy day in April. They wanted to see where everything was located, so they were familiar with the building. Phoebe's aunt and uncle, despite all their traveling, had never taken a train. So they had never been in the station and were in awe when they walked into the Great Hall.

While researching they learned that the magnificent Great Hall at Chicago's Union Station was used for elegant special events, receptions and weddings. It was originally designed by famed architect Daniel Burnham and completed in 1925. It has always been considered one of the greatest indoor spaces in the United States.

Just like her aunt and uncle, people are astonished when they enter this 20,000 square foot classic Beaux Arts style room. The expanse has eighteen soaring Corinthian columns, terracotta walls, a pink Tennessee marble floor and a spectacular five-story, barrel-vaulted, atrium ceiling.

The rich history and beauty of the Great Hall has made it a popular location for movies including *The Untouchables*, *My Best Friend's Wedding*, *Flags of Our Fathers* and many others. It was truly a site everyone should see when first visiting Union Station. Phoebe was not disappointed by her aunt and uncle's reaction to the room.

As they made their way through the Hall and down another ramp they entered the hustle and bustle of the station. With several long distance trains coming and going within a three hour window, there seemed to be people everywhere; some of them pushing and shoving to get to their destination.

Besides the people, there were large sized golf carts with seating for six and a cart attached for luggage, beeping their horns as the Sky Caps tried to move handicapped travelers from one area to another. The noise all around them almost assaulted their senses.

Crossing from one large area to another smaller one they saw the sign for the First Class Lounge and entered through the double doors. Almost immediately the noise was no longer audible. They checked in and found an area in the back of the room to settle down and wait for the call to board.

There were quite a few people in the room. If you traveled in a bedroom or roomette you were allowed into the lounge. There was WiFi, a television with CNN on, drinks and snacks and a bathroom for the first class passengers. But the best part of the room was the overall quietness. Phoebe realized again how noisy it was outside the first class lounge, when she left to meet Tony and Hugh to direct them to where the others were sitting.

The excitement was definitely building for everyone waiting for their respective trains. Finally they announced that the Zephyr was in the station and ready for boarding. Since first class boarded before the other passengers, there were less rude people trying to get to their cars. As the whistles shrieked as various trains clattered up to their platforms, there was a sense of urgency to "get aboard."

Lights shone down on them as they walked through the underground cave like platform to their train. People trying to get to their cars jostled and pushed the six of them. Being in such a hurry was rather silly since everyone walking to the train at this time had their own rooms. They were not vying for a particular seat as the coach passengers had to.

Todd had explained to Phoebe and she had told the others about the "consist" of the train. "Consist" meant the way the cars were placed. At the front were two engines since they would be crossing mountains. Next came the baggage car, three coaches, a lounge car, dining car, two sleeper cars and one dorm car where the service crew slept.

The sleeper cars were separated from the coach cars by the dining and lounge cars to give the first class passengers privacy from the coach travelers. If there were any special Pullman cars, they were at the end. As they walked along the platform the first car they spotted was their Pullman.

They also spied a man and a woman of African-American descent standing at the car. They were dressed in similar outfits—navy blue pants, white shirts, and navy blue vests. The man was wearing a red bow tie, and the woman had a red scarf tied around her neck.

They realized this was Charles, their attendant, who was waiting by the steps to greet them as the other passengers pressed on. Margaret, their cook, was standing next to him. As they ascended the stairs, they introduced themselves. Charles reassured them their luggage was on board, and that as soon as they entered the car he would deliver the bags to the correct rooms.

"Welcome aboard everyone," he said as they climbed up into the Pullman.

Since they still had about twenty minutes before the train left the station they all went to their rooms to drop off their carry-ons and wait for their luggage. They agreed that as soon as they got their bags they would meet in the parlor to watch the train leave the station.

Phoebe could not believe the reality had finally arrived. Her heart picked up speed as the train lurched and with the whistle blowing began pulling out of the tunnel and into the sunlight of downtown Chicago. Although they would be making stops, the twenty-four hundred mile, fifty one hour journey to the west coast was beginning. Even though they would only be on this particular train for one night Phoebe hoped no one was in a hurry, because the train often ran late. Enjoy the journey, she thought to herself. I know I will.

As they sat in the parlor watching the city roll by, Charles came with champagne for everyone.

"I thought you would like to toast your journey," he told them all.

"What an excellent idea," Aunt Julia remarked.

It was not very long before the train left the urban areas behind, as it crossed the open prairie of central Illinois, went over the Mississippi River, and chugged into southern Iowa. Phoebe did not know how it happened but the train was an hour late by the time they arrived in Ottumwa, Iowa, famous as the home to the character Corporal Radar O'Reilly of the television MASH show.

As they made their way up to the dome car for dinner, Charles told them not to worry. Since Amtrak did not own the tracks, they often had to pull over for freight trains. However they also had time built into their schedule, so a lot of the delays could be made up.

They had not said anything about seating arrangements for meals, but as they sat it seemed to just fall in place. Phoebe and Riley took one side of the first table on the right, and the men sat across from them. At the other booth across the aisle to the left, Aunt Julia and Uncle Henry sat on separate sides of each other, with Julia on the same side as the women and Henry as the men. Even though the tables were separated, they were close enough they felt like they were eating together with the women on one side and the men on the other.

As Charles served a wonderful meal of salad, beef bourguignon, twice baked potatoes and a spinach casserole Hugh said, "If we keep eating like this, we will all put on twenty pounds. Good thing we are getting off for a few days tomorrow."

Phoebe started disagreeing until Charles brought Brandy Alexander's, a rich ice cream drink for dessert.

"Don't expect this drink very often," he told the group. "We have limited space for ice cream so I usually serve these after a station stop when we add to our food supplies."

As the sun set over the horizon, the six of them watched the white clouds transform into bright shades of purple and pink while they sipped their drinks.

After dinner they all went to their rooms. They still had not unpacked and tomorrow morning they would be in Denver and getting off for a few days. Phoebe had already packed her clothes so that her suitcase had the things she needed for the Colorado adventure. Because of this it did not take her long to unpack and slip the suitcases under her bed.

She was not used to drinking so much, since she had the champagne on departure, wine with her meal, and the Brandy Alexander for dessert. She did not look out the window very long as twilight descended. She was not sure, if it was the alcohol or the swaying motion of the train, but she was very quickly lulled into a deep sleep.

Chapter 8

There was a time change before Denver and since everyone had gone to sleep early the night before, they were all up at the crack of dawn. The scenery had definitely changed since they went to sleep. There were rolling hills with tumbleweeds blowing around and not a lot of grass. Small little towns quickly appeared and disappeared approximately every hour. As they ate breakfast they spied a herd of antelopes on the vast plains.

Antelopes are the fastest land mammals in North America. They look like deer with white spots but are actually in the goat family. Even though they can run at speeds up to 60 mph, they hate to jump. They would rather dig under a fence than go over it.

As they got closer to Denver the outline of the Rocky Mountains could be seen and Tony pointed out Pikes Peak in the distance.

"Just think. In a few hours we will be at the top of that mountain," he said.

They all felt his excitement as he started telling them a little about the history.

"Pikes Peak is one of Colorado's fifty-eight 'fourteeners.' Those are mountains that rise more than 14,000 feet. There are only ninety-one in all of North America. With nineteen in Alaska that only leaves thirteen in the other Western states. So that it is a pretty impressive number for one state. Pikes Peak is designated a National Historic Landmark and is made up of pink granite."

He continued, "The first Europeans to discover Pikes Peak were the Spanish in the 1700s. Zebulon Pike's expedition was the first American sighting in 1806. Pike had been sent to explore after President Thomas Jefferson sent Lewis and Clark to the Pacific. He mostly explored Iowa, Nebraska and parts of Colorado. Pike failed to climb to the top in November 1806. I can just imagine how bad the weather would have been there at that time of the year."

"I did not realize Pike never made it to the top," Aunt Julia said.

"Most people don't know that. It was fourteen years after Pike that Edwin James, a recent botany college graduate, actually climbed to the top with two other men in two days. He was the first to describe the blue columbine, Colorado's state flower. Then in 1858 Julia and James Holmes reached the summit in August making her the first woman to climb the mountain."

As everyone listened to the rest of his narration, Tony added, "Thirty-five years later, in July 1893, Katherine Lee Bates, a college professor spending the summer in Colorado, wrote the words for the song *America the Beautiful* after admiring the view from the top. There is a plaque at the top commemorating that event."

"Thanks, Tony," Riley said. "That was pretty interesting. I hope I do as well telling everyone about Yosemite when we get there."

Laughing at her remark Hugh said, "Tony is always teaching me new things. He has been doing it since we were kids, and I guess I have taken him for granted for years. We are only on day two, and I can already tell this is going to be an exceptional journey."

"The only thing I am a little sad about is leaving this train so soon," Phoebe pointed out. "It seems like we just got on, and now we are jumping off for a few days. And I slept so well last night. You know it would be very easy to get used to this form of travel. Unfortunately you would have to be a millionaire to keep doing it."

"You would probably need more than a million," Uncle Henry pointed out. "But you are right. As much as I am looking forward to this Colorado adventure, I could easily have spent a few more days on board the train."

They all laughed while agreeing with him.

As they chugged closer to the city the mountain range seemed to go straight up. It was as if everything got vertical very quickly. That fact always amazed Tony when it happened. They had been climbing gradually the last few hours so even though they were at almost five thousand feet, they could not tell they were at that elevation. When he told the group what he was thinking, they all concurred with him.

It was not too long after that the train started backing into Denver's Union Station. Charles had been correct.

They had made up some of their time and they were only a half hour later than the scheduled arrival.

Everyone was ready, and with suitcases in hand descended the stairs of their car. Several people walking by looked at them enviously. They knew how these people were feeling because at times they could barely believe they were on this odyssey.

The rental company was only a couple of blocks from the station and after retrieving their van, they were on their way. Tony drove and Hugh rode shotgun with maps in hand. As they got close to Colorado Springs, they saw the majestic church spire that was the symbol of the Air Force Academy.

Continuing on they soon pulled into the Visitor Center at Garden of the Gods. They saw a short introductory movie about the history of the area and were surprised to learn that, although it took millions of years this was the second set of Rocky Mountains. The first ones were limestone and had eroded down to nothing and then earthquakes and volcanoes had produced this set of granite rocks they were now viewing.

Eating a quick lunch at an outside picnic table while overlooking the park, they read the information about the park's history. The red rock formations were created millions of years ago during a geological upheaval along a natural fault line. Archaeological evidence showed that prehistoric people visited Garden of the Gods about 1330 BC, and about 250 BC Native American people camped in the park.

"I guess you never really think about people actually

being in America that long ago," Riley said. "It says in 1879 Charles Perkins purchased several hundred acres which included a portion of the present day park. Imagine waking up every morning and looking out seeing these beautiful red and pink rocks. It says he wanted to donate the land for a park, but did not have time to set it up in his will before he died. However his family honored his wishes and gave the land to the City of Colorado Springs in 1909. The only provision was that it would always remain a free public park."

As they finished eating Tony said, "Let's jump in the van and get going. This is a one-way drive and I know everyone can see *Kissing Camels* across the road. But just wait until we get on the other side where there are so many other formations. A couple of the names are B*alanced Rock* and S*teamboat Rock.*"

After taking a picture in front of B*alanced Rock* they continued out of the park and into Manitou Springs. This was a very rich little city founded by the second sons of the British aristocracy. Since they could not inherit from their fathers, many of them had come to Colorado in the late 1800's to seek their fortune in gold or silver. They still play polo in this town of 8,000 feet.

As they drove to the cog railway Tony said, "Get your jackets out."

"Why do we need our jackets? It is over 70 degrees here."

"But not for long, Riley. When you are at 8,000 feet for every one thousand feet higher you go the temperature drops 10 degrees. Since we will be ascending another 6,000 feet it will be 60 degrees cooler at the top."

"I find that hard to believe," Phoebe chimed in.

"When we get off the cog at the top of the mountain you will remember what I said."

Tony was right. It was only 18 degrees at the top and they were all glad they had jackets. Due to the altitude the six of them felt half drunk as they made their way swaying to the Visitor Center. Riley felt a little sick to her stomach and had some Seven Up. She had been drinking water to stay hydrated but the soda made her feel a lot better. The two men each had a "greasy donut" and Uncle Henry decided he needed a shot of oxygen from one of the canisters located in the building.

The sky could not have been clearer and they knew this was not always a given so they felt very lucky. After taking a picture next to the plaque of Katherine Lee Bates' poem they got back into the "cog" and soon it was making its descent back down the mountain.

They had booked their hotel right downtown and after checking in they had gone to the old train station that was now a restaurant. As freight trains rattled by they had a wonderful meal starting with a salad bar that was served out of an old railroad cart. Everyone decided on the Rocky Mountain trout for their entree and they all decided to skip dessert.

It was not long before they were back in their hotel rooms tucked in for the night. It had been a wonderful day, and tomorrow looked just as promising.

Chapter 9

After breakfast they were on the road by 9:00 a.m. They drove past the Broadmore, a famous luxurious historic hotel. As they started climbing they could see Fort Carson, an army base, on their left. A lot of famous people had been stationed there including Clark Gable during World War II. On the right was Cheyenne Mountain where the government had a not so secret NORAD base built deep into the earth.

They continued on to Canon City, known as prison city, for the thirteen prisons in the area. One of them was a Supermax where Tim McVeigh spent time before he was put to death for his involvement in the Oklahoma City bombing.

The city itself had a very charming appearance. They drove to the train station and picked up their tickets. The personnel were grilling some hot dogs and bratwurst, so they bought sandwiches. The train would be following the Arkansas River through a deep gorge. As they sat eating their food at picnic tables on the patio they spied a small black bear cub on the other side of the river. They hoped his mother was not close by.

The train was a two and a half hour ride following the "Grand Canyon of the Arkansas River." On the way back one could stop and ride a little car to the top of the mountain and walk the famous Hanging Bridge.

Because of time constraints they did not do that stop. They had to drive right by there on their way out of town, so they would decide later if they wanted to make a stop. It was not long before the train pulled into the station. They made sure they were all sitting on the left side, so they could have views of the river on their journey.

Although it seemed a short train ride with beautiful scenery, it had been a wonderful jaunt. As they returned to the station, they were all saying how glad they were that they had taken that train. They stopped briefly at the Hanging Bridge to take a picture from the top. Since they had one hundred forty miles to go until their hotel, they decided to keep moving.

The hotel had a restaurant and rather than going out to eat somewhere, they dined there. It was another early night, but there was a lot to do the next day. It was a half hour ride to Antonito where they would catch the Cumbres & Toltec train.

Tony had lined up a man who was retired from the train to drive their van on to Chama, New Mexico. He was happy to do it since he took any chance he could to ride his beloved train. They paid him a small amount for driving their van and Tony gave him money for lunch when he got to Chama. They also bought his one way ticket back home on the train.

It would take them six hours to get to Chama which

included lunch. On train excursion days, some ladies would ride their 4-wheel drive jeeps up the mountain to prepare a meatloaf or turkey lunch with homemade pies for the passengers.

This was another nice ride on a narrow gauge coal driven train. They had all worn dark clothes so the coal dust would not show. Tony mentioned they should wear the same clothes the next day on their next coal train. By the time their ride was over, Riley's red hair looked like it had turned black and she said she was definitely wearing the same clothes tomorrow.

"No use getting another outfit full of coal dust," she said.

They were high up in the mountains at over 10,000 feet when they stopped for lunch. Phoebe loved the area, because instead of jagged peaks the hills were rounded. She knew they would be going though jagged peaks the next day and liked the idea of the contrast of the two rides.

It took a little over two hours to go from Chama to Durango. Both Riley and Phoebe were disappointed they had not decided to stay an extra day in Durango. It was a typical small Western town in the mountains. She would have liked some shopping time in the town and when she learned Mesa Verde, an Anasazi site, was nearby she was sorry they had not included another day in this area.

They stayed in an old Western hotel a block from the train station. It was supposedly haunted, but no one saw any evidence of it that night. They found a wonderful steakhouse and saloon across the street from their hotel for dinner.

The next day they were up early, and wearing the same clothes they boarded the Durango & Silverton train. This ride was listed as one of the top 10 train rides in the world and with the jagged vistas and mountain peaks they all understood why. However it was hard to say you liked one train better than the other since the scenery was so different. They were all glad they had the opportunity to ride both trains.

Tony had found a volunteer who was not riding the train that day to take their van to Silverton. He declined any pay, but took some lunch money and his free ticket home. Since the ride by train was four hours, but only one hour by vehicle the man, whose name was Jake, told Tony he would not leave Durango until 10:30 a.m.

Silverton was a very small cute mining town. The mines had long been played out and if it was not for the tourists, it would be a ghost town. It ran about four blocks with saloons on either side of the street, an old hotel, restaurants and shops.

The train stopped right in the middle of the street as it chugged into town. Jake was waiting near the platform with the keys. He pointed out where he had parked the van. The street was pretty crowded with tourists and Jake recommended a restaurant that had good food and fast service. He thanked everyone for letting him help them out and was quickly on his way. He knew he had another hour and a half before his train would head home, so he headed to a nearby restaurant to have lunch with some friends.

After lunch they quickly got into the van. A little more time in this cute little town would have been fun, but they wanted to catch their train. As they left Silverton, Tony continued driving and Riley asked if she could sit in the front seat with him. Aunt Julia and Uncle Henry liked the third seat in the back, so that is where they sat. That put Phoebe and Hugh in the middle seat.

Phoebe asked Hugh how he and Riley had met. He told her the story, as they drove the twenty-four mile stretch of mountain road called the "Million Dollar Highway." Supposedly there was so much gold and silver dust that was used in making the road, that it was given that name. However others said it cost a million to build. No matter what the reason for the name it was twenty-four miles of switchbacks at fifteen to twenty mph and a bit treacherous.

Most people driving the road have white knuckles traversing that section into the town of Ouray. As they came down off the mountain the town lay straight out in front of them. Ouray was another one of those old mining towns and one of the mine owners years ago had struck it so rich he bought his daughter the Hope Diamond.

As they passed several cute towns along the way, one with hot springs, Phoebe told Tony she wished they had more time to stop along the way.

Answering her while he drove Tony said, "There are so many neat little towns in this area, Phoebe. I spent a whole summer exploring this state and probably missed a few places. It would be fun making a few stops, but then we would probably miss our train."

"I definitely don't want to do that. I think, as much fun as this has been, everyone is looking forward to getting back on our Pullman," Phoebe said.

Laughing Tony replied, "And the first thing everyone will want to do is take a shower and wash the coal dust from their hair."

"You are definitely right about that," she agreed.

They arrived at the station and discovered the train was only running a half hour late. Tony, who had lined up the rental vans, had made arrangements for an employee at the rental car company to pick up their van. A special envelop had been left with the station master for Tony to put the keys in. That way when he had some time, the driver could pick up the keys and take the van back to the lot after they departed.

It was not very long, before they heard the whistle. The train was almost at the station, and they were all filled with excitement. As they stood on the platform, suitcases in hand, they knew they had a wonderful Colorado adventure but they were looking forward to their next overnight in the Pullman.

Chapter 10

It felt so good to be back on the train. They did not have the space they had in a hotel room, but it felt cozy and inviting. They were now traveling through Red Rock country. As they left Grand Junction heading towards Salt Lake City, Utah, the Book Cliff Mountains could be seen on the right. The land on the left, once containing a lot of uranium, was a high desert area filled with red soil.

There was nothing to see for miles except this landscape. Since the train rapidly reached seventy miles per hour Phoebe thought if someone was standing outside, the thunder and noise of the train would sound like hundreds of buffaloes stampeding. She was sure they would feel the ground shake. And after the train went by there would be a silence that was almost deafening.

It was just a couple of hours ago they were in the mountains, and now this desert region which looked so totally different. They had been viewing Ponderosa Pines and Blue Spruce, and now there was not a tree in sight. The way the scenery changed as they travelled across the country was amazing.

It was roughly 5:15 p.m. when the train left the station. After unpacking and taking showers, everyone congregated in the parlor for a glass of wine about an hour later.

At 7:00 p.m. Charles announced dinner was served and they made their way up to the dome car. Tonight chicken was on the menu, and as usual Margaret's meal was outstanding.

As they watched the desert whiz by Phoebe heard a sharp voice say, "Aren't you going to finish your dinner, Riley? It is not good to waste food like that."

"Hugh, please leave her alone," Tony said.

At that Hugh got up and saying he was skipping dessert said good night.

"What was that all about?" Riley asked Tony. "I don't waste food but my stomach is a little upset so I decided not to finish my dinner. I did not think that would offend anyone."

"Ignore him Riley. Hugh's wife had some food issues. This is the anniversary of her death and I think he was upset and did not realize what he was saying. I know he will be very embarrassed tomorrow when he sees you."

"It really was rather strange. Hugh and I have been friends for awhile and gone out together quite a few times. He has never said anything like that before. We had such a great time in Colorado, but I am a little tired and since my stomach is upset, I think I will also skip dessert. Good night, everyone."

As Riley left Uncle Henry said, "You can count me in for dessert." Phoebe's aunt smiled at them when her husband made that statement.

At that point Charles came up to remove their plates while bringing a tray filled with plates of banana cream pie.

"Aunt Julia, would you mind if I just took a couple of bites out of your pie? I don't think I can eat a whole piece. That chicken dinner was really filling."

"That's fine, dear. I don't need a whole piece either despite what your uncle says."

After dinner Tony went down to the parlor to read his book. The rest of them decided to go to their rooms. Phoebe also had a good book, but she liked reading in the comfort of her room.

Tomorrow the train would arrive in Reno, Nevada about 8:30 a.m. They would uncouple the Pullman and explore the Reno/Lake Tahoe region for the day. It promised to be another wonderful adventure.

Chapter 11

Tony was correct. The next morning Hugh ran into Riley coming out of her room and turned red seeing her. Apologizing for his behavior the previous evening, she told him it was already forgotten. She did not want him to continue feeling bad. It was important to just move on.

With that they went to the dome car for breakfast. Margaret had made scrambled eggs, fried potatoes, slices of ham and blueberry muffins. As Charles was serving, Riley said, "Charles please tell Margaret she is spoiling us terribly. It will be very difficult to go back home and have to fix all my own food. And it definitely will not taste as good as this does."

At her words the man smiled while saying, "She will be very happy to hear your compliment, Miss Riley."

Soon the other four joined them and they were all chatting about their day. This time Phoebe had planned their itinerary.

"When the train stops Tony will get off and go to get the van. We may as well stay on the Pullman and be comfortable. After they uncouple us Tony should be back with the van, and we can take off. Reno bills itself as "The Biggest Little City In The World" and we will probably see the sign that says that. Since we are still in the high desert it can be quite warm, but always cools down at night."

She continued, "The population is a little over 225,000 making it the second largest city in the state. Just to the west of Reno are the Sierra Nevada Mountains and they are quite spectacular. We will drive into them going to Lake Tahoe and also tomorrow on the train ride to Sacramento."

"Is there anything to see downtown?"

"Not really, Hugh. There are some gambling resort hotels, but unlike Las Vegas there is no glitz here. Actually Indian gaming in California and Oregon has brought a downturn in the town's economy. The University of Nevada–Reno is located in the city and the National Bowling Stadium which brings in conventions. There is also a National Automobile Museum. In the past there were dude ranches and many women came and stayed for six weeks to establish residency to get divorces. But that practice no longer exists."

"Why did we decide to stop here?" Hugh asked.

"Because not too far from here is Lake Tahoe, the second deepest lake in the US and sixteenth in the world. We will go there later this afternoon, as we will be making a big circle. First we will go up to Virginia City. Next we will drive through Carson City, the capital. Finally we will take a steep mountain road to the lake. When we leave Lake Tahoe there is the town of Truckee, an old Western railroad town with lots of charm. Since the train goes through there, we probably won't stop. However, just so you know, only two miles from Truckee is the Donner Memorial State Park. That is where eighty nine people died and were eaten by the remaining party members in order to survive during the winter of 1846-47."

"So what is important about Virginia City," Riley asked?

"Carson City was founded in 1858 and became the capitol in 1864. At the time Nevada did not have enough population to be a state, but President Lincoln overrode that. He was fighting a war and needed the silver coming out of the Comstock Lode in Virginia City, fifteen miles northeast to make bullets."

She continued, "In the 1870s with almost 30,000 residents, more than 100 saloons, many banks, churches, theaters and the only elevator between Chicago and San Francisco that mining metropolis ran twenty-four hours a day. Mark Twain and Bret Harte worked as reporters for the newspaper. Today if it was not for tourism, Virginia City would be a ghost town. But many of the buildings have been preserved and we can visit the Delta Casino and Saloon where we will see the Suicide Table, Comstock Fireman's Museum, Mackay Mansion, Piper's Opera House, the Bucket of Blood Saloon, and the Silver Queen Saloon and Hotel. There is a 15 foot tall dress made of 3200 silver dollars, and a belt made of $5 gold pieces on display. Supposedly it is a climb in and out of the mountains to get there, but well worth the trek."

"We will probably just drive through Carson City but we should see the Capitol Building with its silver dome. The federal government established a mint for coining the silver. I have a friend who says the Nevada State Museum is also an interesting attraction," Tony added.

"The problem is we could have spent an extra day in this area but with so many sights on out trip, we have to be a little selective, Tony."

"You're right, Phoebe. So what can you tell us about the lake?"

"South Lake Tahoe is where the majority of people go. You can take a cruise on the lake to Emerald Bay to see a castle called Vikingsholm, a reproduction of a ninth century Norse fortress. But most people come to this area for the water sports and in the winter the excellent nearby ski runs. The majority of the lake is in Nevada, but part is in California. Due to time constraints we won't go to South Lake Tahoe."

"Will we miss anything by not going there?" Riley asked.

"No. From what I have read the whole lake is a deep emerald green from the glaciers that went through and ponderosa pines are everywhere. We will enter on the eastern side about two-thirds down and go north There is a place along the way that has the former set from the Bonanza television show. Then we will enter a little town called Incline Village. I read Leonard Nimoy had a home there. The whole region we will be in is called North Lake Tahoe."

"Is that where the Cal-Neva is located?"

"Yes, Tony it is. And it has recently reopened after a major renovation. I thought we could stop there for a bathroom break. Just so the rest of you know it was once owned by Frank Sinatra and in its heyday the Rat Pack partied hard there. One room had a stage and I'll bet there were some wild parties on New Year's Eve, and whenever else they went there. Marilyn Monroe even had her own cottage. There is another room with a large fireplace where the two state lines pass through. We might be able to straddle the two sides and take pictures while we are standing in the two states at the same time. From there we will head to the interstate near Truckee and go east back to Reno."

"What are our plans for dinner?"

"I talked to Charles about that, Riley. Obviously we will be eating lunch out somewhere. He said Margaret will make a hotdish that just needs to be warmed up. When we get back to the interstate near Truckee I will call him, so he has an estimate of what time we will be back. Then Margaret can pop the food in the microwave for us."

"That sounds like a great idea," Riley concluded.

By 9:30 a.m. they were in the van and leaving Reno. They had a wonderful day, and Hugh's outburst the night before had been forgotten. They went to Virginia City, and then on to Carson City. They did not stop at the museum because of time constraints.

Knowing there would be no place to eat until North Lake Tahoe, which would be later in the afternoon, they stopped at a grocery store in Carson City. They bought premade sandwiches, chips, cookies, apples and bottled water. They found a perfect spot overlooking the lake to have a picnic lunch.

They arrived back at the Pullman by 8:00 p.m. Eating

their hotdish while talking about the day, they were in their rooms by 9:00 p.m. There were two exceptions. Tony once again went to the parlor to read, and Riley stayed in the dome car to review her notes for Yosemite.

Tomorrow they would be spending the night in Sacramento and then the next night in the park. After that San Francisco would beckon. No one could believe how quickly the trip was flying by.

Chapter 12

It was just past 10:00 p.m. when Tony closed his book. He knew Riley was still up in the dome car so he decided to go see what she was up to. He smiled when he saw her at the research table, her back to him, poring over maps, books, and brochures.

She was startled when she heard, "Riley, aren't you going to bed soon?"

"You surprised me, Tony. I thought everyone was asleep."

Sliding in across from her he picked up a brochure on Yosemite. "How did you get this? I thought they only gave these brochures out when you visit the park?"

"They do give them out at all the parks, but I wrote ahead for this one in the spring. It has all the essential information we need and a wonderful park map inside."

Showing him the map she said, "See we will be coming into the park from the north and then go out the west entrance. I have also mapped out your route from Sacramento as well as to Oakland."

"That was very thoughtful of you. I planned to use the GPS on my phone but I also like paper copies to look at."

"I know I do, too. A GPS is great but I am a visual learner and like having a map as a backup. I know young people today would probably laugh at me."

"I have never thought about it but you are absolutely right. Kids would probably laugh at us for using maps. But don't you think it is time to turn in?"

"Yes it is. I was just finishing up. You gave us such wonderful information when we were in Colorado and Phoebe did really great yesterday in the Reno area. I don't want to fall down on the job. It was my idea to go to Yosemite. I have heard so much about it and I wanted my information to be good, too."

"I am sure whatever you tell us will be great. On another note, I know Hugh and I have really enjoyed traveling with you and Phoebe. I am not used to being around women as friends. I know Hugh has often said what a nice person you are. But can I ask you a personal question?"

"Sure. My life is an open book."

" Hugh told me you had a great marriage. So why haven't you remarried?"

Blushing she said, "You will probably think this sounds crazy but I did have a wonderful marriage. I got married when I was twenty-four and we were very happy for thirty-one years. Jake got blood clots while traveling and died at the emergency room door, as I was taking him to the hospital. I used to think if only I had gotten him to the hospital a few minutes sooner, he might still be alive.

Actually that is how I met Phoebe."

"She was at the hospital where your husband died?"

"Oh, no. Sorry. I did not mean to confuse you. I went to grief counseling and we met in the therapist's office one morning and became good friends. Her husband had Alzheimer's. Between the time it took for him to be diagnosed and taking care of him until he died, almost ten years went by. Therapy helped her come to terms with all she went through. Now she goes around to a lot of Alzheimer's groups to speak about her experience."

"It is really great that she does that. Hugh and I volunteer two days a week at a foster children's residence. We could not meet with you on Thursdays and Fridays because those are the days we volunteer. There are not enough foster homes for all the kids who need them so we have a friend who opened a temporary facility in a mansion he owns until foster homes can be found for the children."

"Is that why you asked Phoebe if she liked kids?"

"Yes. I never had children of my own and these kids need help so desperately. I would find it hard to like someone who did not like children. But you still did not answer the question of why you did not remarry."

"Like you, I never had a chance to have children. For some reason it never happened for Jake and me. We had such a happy life and were so busy, we never dwelled on it."

She continued, "It's been three years since Jake died. At first I was shell shocked that he was gone so quickly. Then I settled into a routine without him. My therapist really helped with that. But I keep thinking since we had such an amazing marriage, how could a second one be as good. And it would be difficult to go through that pain again. So it is better to just have friends. I don't know Hugh's story but we have enjoyed going out together because neither one of us wants a commitment."

"Maybe someday I will tell you Hugh's story. He was married to a woman who died from anorexia. It was very difficult dealing with someone who refused to admit she had a problem while watching her waste away. Hugh went to therapy for awhile like you because he blamed himself. It took him a long time to realize it was not his fault."

"That is terrible. I feel so bad for him. No wonder he jumped me the other night about not eating. He did not know I wasn't feeling well."

"And it was the fourth anniversary of Hillary's death. That day is always difficult for him. So are you ready to turn in now?"

"Not so fast. I told you my story, and now I want to hear yours."

"I guess that is only fair. As you know Hugh and I have been friends all our lives. We grew up in the same neighborhood and went to the same college. We met the women we married in college. I got married at twenty-one when we graduated and Hugh the following year. So all four of us were close friends."

He then continued, "I was married to Ginger for fourteen years   Although I made pretty good money we were not wealthy. Ginger did not want to work. All she ever wanted was to be a mother. We tried for seven years. Finally she went to a doctor to see if there was something wrong with her. There was. The doctor said we would never have children."

"That must have been terrible for the two of you."

"Yes it was. But I accepted it. I told her we could adopt but she refused. I realized for some reason I was not meant to have children. But, unlike you, Ginger could not accept the reality. She became very depressed and started drinking. She finally eased up on the drinking and I thought things were getting better. Instead she started hoarding, and our garage became loaded with newspapers, magazines, and unopened boxes of I don't know what. It seemed harmless and I thought if it made her happy, it was not such a big deal. Then we had a fire in the garage and lost everything. She was inconsolable."

"That had to be tragic for her."

"It was but that was not the worst part. I did not realize that she had become a compulsive spender. All those unopened boxes in the garage were items she had bought. She had taken out several credit cards and spent her day watching the home shopping channels. I was at work during the day so I never saw what was being delivered. After the fire she gave me her credit card bills. She had charged over $45,000.00. I told her she had to get help, but she refused. She divorced me instead. Not only did I have to pay her alimony but it took me three years, after getting settlement agreements, to pay off all the credit card debts. And with nothing to show for it."

Shocked at what he had told her Riley said, "I just don't know what to say. What a terrible experience you went through. No wonder you never married again. What happened to Ginger?"

"It was really sad. She moved in with her sister and used the alimony money I sent her to buy drugs. I don't know all the details but she died of a drug overdose three years after we divorced. She was only thirty eight years old. What a wasted life, and all because she refused to get help and learn to accept what she could not change."

"Oh my gosh. That is such a sad story."

"It doesn't bother me like it used to. I have a wonderful support group of friends. And I get a lot of pleasure from my volunteering. It is hard to believe I have been divorced for twenty eight years, and Ginger has been gone twenty five. I often think of all the wonderful things that have happened to me over the years that she missed out on."

Frowning he continued, "But enough of all that. I want you to know I would not mind going out with you as a friend if you are not busy with Hugh. It would be so nice to have someone who isn't trying to get me to marry them. I rarely go out anymore except in a group situation, because so many women I have dated insisted on me taking the relationship to the next level. And I have always told them up front that I am only interested in being friends."

"I would love being your friend. That is the reason I have only gone out with Hugh. He places no demands on me and I worry other men might not act the same way. "

Yawning he said, "Bedtime. You will do fine tomorrow. But first we have some beautiful sites to see in the Sierra Nevada Mountains along the way and you need to get your beauty rest."

Smiling at him she put her research materials back in the box, and the two descended the stairs to their rooms.

Chapter 13

The sun was shining brightly as they gathered for breakfast. The Ponderosa Pine trees surrounded them, and the scenery was breathtaking. After Truckee they passed Donner Lake where the immigrants had resorted to cannibalism.

The Zephyr had a route guide, and they followed along as their journey continued. After passing the lake, the train went through tunnels and a series of snow sheds. These sheds protected the track from being blocked by the more than 30 feet of snow that falls in a typical winter.

As they were eating lunch Charles pointed out Castle Peak, a mountain that looked like it had a castle on top. They also crossed the old pioneer trail and in one area the cliffs were so steep, Charles told them the pioneers had to lower their wagons on ropes to continue their trek.

Then it was on to Colfax, the heart of gold country. A statue at the station was a prospector panning for gold during the Gold Rush days of the 1850s. They could almost see all the miners and their mules trudging along the paths looking for a place where they could pan for gold.

As they ate lunch Riley told them about Sacramento and a little background on Yosemite. "Since we are staying overnight, you may want to know a little bit about Sacramento, California's state capital. The city was first settled in 1839. Naturally, the city grew significantly during the California Gold Rush, and in 1854 became the capital. The city was the western terminus for the Pony Express and this afternoon we are staying right next to Old Town. The city was also the starting point for eastbound construction to meet the westbound track of the first transcontinental railroad at Promontory Point in Utah in 1869. The California State Railroad Museum is there which is very appropriate."

"Wasn't it John Sutter, of the gold fame, who settled the town?" Uncle Henry asked. "I think he settled on the American River near its confluence with the Sacramento River. It was a perfect spot because not only were the rivers the roads in the old days, but water was important for their survival."

"Yes you are right about that. And from what I can determine online they still have a lot of the old pioneer buildings and wooden sidewalks. In the 1960s they redeveloped the area and it became the first historic district created in the West. Our hotel is right on the edge of the district. We walk through a tunnel, and we are there. And the railroad museum is only a couple of blocks from our hotel."

"Julia and I have been there before and it is quite a place. The museum first opened in 1976 and people from around the world come to experience this world-renowned attraction. There are six buildings but the main building has twenty-one restored locomotives and cars. There are numerous exhibits that show how the railroads shaped people's lives at that time. They even have a Pullman-style sleeping car, a dining car filled with railroad china, and a Railway Post Office that you can go through. I am really looking forward to visiting again."

"Tony made arrangements to have the van waiting for us at the station, so it won't take long to get to Old Town. Since the museum closes at 5:00 p.m. we will go directly there. At least that should give us about two hours to experience the place. Then we can go check in to our hotel and walk back over to Old Town. We can browse through the shops before dinner. Does that sound all right to everyone?"

Since they all agreed with Riley's plan, she started telling them about Yosemite. "It will take us about three and one half hours just to get to the Park, so I think we should be on the road by 8:00 a.m. Yosemite's elevations start at just under 3,000 feet and rise as high as 13,000 feet, so we have a steep climb from the valley floor to get there. That will slow us down."

As they listened she continued, "The future park was first protected in 1864. It is best known for its waterfalls, deep valleys, beautiful meadows, ancient giant sequoias, and a vast wilderness area. Over 95% of the park is wilderness. The main part of the action is in Yosemite Valley where the hotels and campsites are located. That is also where we are headed."

Everyone was listening intently because they knew how hard she had worked to research the area.

"The park was designated a World Heritage Site in

1984. Most of the trees are the Western Red Cedars, which we call Sequoias, and the Ponderosa Pine Trees that are over three hundred years old. There are not many places left in our country today where you can see old growth forests like that. There are two rivers, the Tuolumne and Merced, which begin in the park and flow west to the Central Valley."

Continuing she added, "Humans have lived there for thousands of years, but the rugged terrain challenged many of those early travelers who came by horseback or stagecoach. By 1907, construction of the Yosemite Valley Railroad from Merced to El Portal eased the journey increasing visitation. It was John Muir who got the place designated as a national park in 1890. And Ansel Adam's photographs also made it popular."

"You really studied up on your history, Riley."

"There is a lot more to tell you, Phoebe, but since we are taking the tram tour tomorrow I think the only thing else you need to know is about our hotel tomorrow night. As you know it is called the Ahwahnee. It is quite unique from the other lodges that were built with materials found in their locales. All natural resources in National Parks are protected now, and building materials cannot be used from the parks any more. Since the lodge was not built until 1926, trucks had to haul all the building materials in over primitive roads seven days a week. The primary building materials were steel, granite and concrete. The outside granite and concrete was stained to look like redwood."

"I have seen pictures of the lodge, and just assumed it was made from the wood in the forest there."

"That makes it pretty amazing doesn't it Hugh? It was used as a rest and relaxation place for wounded soldiers during World War II with over 90,000 troops sent there. When we drive up we will see a central tower several stories tall and three separate wings with huge fireplaces. The west wing has a dining room that seats 350 people. The room is one hundred thirty feet long, over fifty-one feet wide and the ceiling reaches thirty-four feet.   It is a massive room and very beautiful."

As she finished talking about the hotel, Tony started clapping and said, "That was excellent, Riley. I know how hard you worked on you research, and I know I speak for everyone when I say what a great job you did."

Blushing as the others all agreed with him, she smiled at Tony and winked at him.

Chapter 14

Once again they climbed down the steps of the Pullman with suitcases in hand. They waved good-bye to Charles and Margaret who were going on to Emeryville, the last Zephyr stop on the way to San Francisco.

Their van was waiting for them and they drove off to the Railroad Museum. Everything went according to plan and after they checked into their hotel they strolled the streets of Old Town and had dinner.

The hotel had a continental breakfast and they met in the lobby at 7:00 a.m. They all loved the fact they were an on time group and found themselves in the van and on their way by 7:45 a.m. They got to Yosemite Valley by 1:00 p.m. and since they could not check into the hotel until after 4:00 p.m. they decided to change their tram tour time.

They were able to get on the 2:30 p.m. tram. They had a quick lunch in the cafeteria located in the area and marveled at the sites they could see from the valley. As it was early in the season and the snow was still melting, the water coming off Yosemite Falls was spectacular.

Taking the tram early had worked out really well. They were able to sign up for a ranger program that evening, and a ranger led hike the next morning, before they would leave the park. But first they had the tour.

They all thought they had learned a lot from Riley but they found out even more as the tram took them around to the famous sites in the valley. The guide told them the park has over 3.5 million visitors a year. As they started their tour the first stop was El Capitan, the 3,000 foot monolith. It is one of the world's favorite challenges for rock climbers.

The guide told them people can only climb up and then must take the trail back down because it is so dangerous. Right near El Capitan they gazed at the 2,425-foot Yosemite Falls, the tallest waterfall in North America. Across from El Capitan there were some other granite monolith rocks, such as Half Dome. These rocks were carved out by the glaciers that came through the area.

As the tram continued they went passed some meadows filled with wildflowers before entering a tunnel. They learned the tunnel was constructed by the WPA in 1933. However as people came out of the tunnel there were so many accidents that the Overlook became a very dangerous place to pull over. So the Tunnel View Overlook was renovated and re-dedicated in 2008.

The Tunnel View Scenic Overlook is an historic region. They discovered it had beautiful views of Yosemite Valley, El Capitan, Bridalveil Falls, and Half Dome. Both the Wawona Tunnel and Tunnel View were determined as eligible for listing on the National Register of Historic Places in 1986 because of their exemplary designs. The guide said the overlook is such a popular site that there is an estimated 5,000 to 7,000 people who visit every day during the height of the tourist season. Even more special was when the tram pulled off onto the Overlook. They walked to the end of the parking lot and the way the sun was positioned they could see a large rainbow over the distant Bridalveil Falls. It was an incredible site to behold, and it took their breath away.

"Wow. I can't thank you enough Riley for suggesting we come to Yosemite," Tony said. "I think I will remember this place until the day I die."

As usual the others nodded in agreement.

After the tram tour they checked into the hotel. The interior, which had beamed ceilings and a massive stone hearth, was done in a Native American décor. Their rooms were wonderful and had fireplaces in the two rooms that shared the balcony. They ordered a bottle of wine from room service, and invited the men over to sit on their balcony. They talked about their day, as they sipped their wine.

They had a wonderful dinner in the dining room and everyone went to the ranger talk. Aunt Julia said if she got tired she could sleep on the car ride to Oakland the next day. She and Uncle Henry had never been to this park and wanted to experience everything.

The older couple did pass on the hike the next morning, and opted to sit on their balcony after breakfast. It was 11:00 a.m. when they checked out of the hotel. They knew it would take them a good five hours to get back to the Pullman.

Tony was still driving and he asked Hugh if it was okay for Riley to sit up front with him. "I know I have my GPS, but Riley has mapped the route back to Oakland. She can keep an eye out on these winding roads to make sure we are headed correctly."

Hugh nodding his head climbed into the second seat with Phoebe. Everyone was pretty quiet on the drive. They stopped in a little town along the way for lunch, and Tony topped off the gas tank. As promised, Aunt Julia and Uncle Henry napped after lunch.

At one point Tony's GPS told him to take a road that was different from the one Riley had mapped out. Although his route looked faster, Riley had read there was construction in that direction and suggested an alternative road. He decided to go with her hunch, and they breezed through the Oakland suburbs missing a lot of afternoon traffic.

It was about 4:00 p.m. when they arrived at the train station. The view wasn't great sitting in a railroad yard but they were glad to be back "home" as they thought of the Pullman.

They had missed a lot of Oakland's rush hour traffic and Tony parked the van in a place that had been set aside for them at the station. Charles was waiting. It took two trips in the golf cart he was using to get them to where the Pullman was parked. Not knowing when they would get to Oakland they had asked Margaret to fix one of her hotdishes for dinner.

They sat in the parlor having their wine and talked about their latest adventure. At 7:00 p.m. Charles called them to dinner. Although the scenery was nothing to look at, they did not seem to notice. They ate Margaret's wonderful concoction and continued talking to each other about the incredible journey they were having.

Chapter 15

It was Day 11, and San Francisco beckoned. It was incredible how fast time was flying by.

"Hugh, we have been friends all our lives, and I want to ask you something about Riley."

Hugh looked at Tony as he sat up in his bed. "Don't tell me she is still upset about me jumping on her the other night about her food?"

"No. It has nothing to do with that. I think that is all forgotten. You have been pretty lucky finding women who just want to be friends. I know you have two or three other lady friends besides Riley."

"That's true. And you always seem to manage to find the ones who want commitments."

"I don't want to take Riley away from you but I asked her if she would mind going out with me on occasion when we get home if she isn't tied up with you. She is definitely not looking for anything serious and was agreeable to my suggestion. But I wanted to make sure you are okay with that."

"My reputation does seem to precede me. For some reason the women I know definitely realize I am not willing to be anything but friends. And unlike you, I have found women who feel the same way. If Riley wants to bum around with you when we get home that is fine with me."

"Thanks, Hugh. We have been friends too long to let a woman come between us. And one more thing. Since I am doing most of the driving, do you think Riley could sit with me in the front seat? I was really impressed with her mapping skills yesterday, and the good advice she gave on that alternate route. I know you dislike maps of any kind."

"That's fine, Tony. There seems to be a lot more leg room by the door in that second seat anyway. And, actually I was talking to Phoebe in the car yesterday after lunch. I am very impressed with how she took care of her husband during his illness. I think she is very brave to go on those speaking engagements in hopes of helping others. She never wants another commitment so I am fine teaming up with her. But I think we should ask the ladies if it is okay with them, if we partner up for the rest of the trip."

Tony, greatly relieved, smiled at his friend as he got up to take a shower.

It was not long after that when everyone met for breakfast. Hugh mentioned their idea to the women and they were both fine with it. Since Riley had some self image issues in the past, she was really pleased that Tony thought highly of her map skills.

"We really do make a good team, don't we?" Phoebe added.

"I know you said it was important to be compatible and

you were right, of course. We have all jelled so quickly. I am a little surprised that it has gone so well."

"I think working together on this trip for three months ahead of time helped us form a bond, Hugh. And giving everyone responsibility for certain areas has helped all of us feel more important to the whole team."

"And now, Tony and I will take over on the San Francisco portion. Do you realize when we leave San Francisco we will have been together for two weeks? The time is going too quickly for me. I am enjoying every single day and don't want this trip to end."

They all agreed with Hugh, as Tony began telling them about their day.

"We will drive across the Oakland Bridge this morning into the Fisherman's Wharf area. I found a parking lot where we can leave the van for the day. Everything in that area is very walkable. First up is a city tour by bus. I already ordered the tickets online."

"By the way," Phoebe added. "That was an excellent suggestion you had, Hugh, about throwing our money into one big pot for tickets and expenses like gas. It is so much easier than constantly asking everyone to throw in their share every time we purchase something."

"I am glad you all agreed. I am using a single credit card and that way I have receipts for everything. It is much less hassle to have a community pot for incidentals," Hugh said as he beamed at her.

"Riley and I thought it was a great idea. We decided to use just one credit card to pay hotels and other personal expenses we are sharing, and then we will also settle up at the end."

"All right now back to our plan for the day. The tour will take us through the Fisherman Wharf area and past Lombard Street, the crookedest street in America. Then we go through the downtown past the Opera House and City Hall before climbing up to Twin Peaks for an overview of the city's skyline. Finally, we head back through Golden Gate Park, the Presidio, and Chinatown before the tour concludes.

After the tour we can take a cable car back to Chinatown for lunch. Then we will do a boat ride on the bay. I am glad everyone opted out of the Alcatraz tour. The boat will take us along the city shoreline, under the Golden Gate Bridge, and finally circle Alcatraz Island before docking. "

Everyone was nodding at Tony as he continued. "Then we will spend some time on Pier 39. It is very touristy but a fun place with lots of shops and restaurants. We will also need to go visit the sea lions. They are on platforms out at the end of the pier and are very noisy with their barking. But it is a San Francisco tradition to see them."

"That sounds like a fun day you have planned," Aunt Julia said. "Henry and I have been here before and I think you have done a great job of picking the most important things to do in such a short amount of time."

"Thank you for the kind words, Julia. It means a lot coming from you, because I know you and Henry have been to all these places before."

Looking at the others he continued, "I have given

Margaret the next two nights off from fixing us dinners. Not only do we want to see things but I think it's crazy to fight rush hour traffic back across the bridge in the evenings just to get back for dinner."

"That's fine with all of us," Riley said as the others agreed. "I am just glad we are able to use our Pullman as our hotel. That would have been an added expense none of us needs."

"If everyone is finished with breakfast, why don't we go get what we need from our rooms and be on our way? It will take Charles two trips on the golf cart to get us to the station where our van is parked."

At that point everyone got up and followed Tony to their rooms.

Chapter 16

It was not long before they were all climbing into their seats in the van. Tony had suggested they wait until 8:30 a.m. to leave to avoid rush hour going into the city. Their three hour city tour was scheduled for 10:00 a.m. That would give them enough time to park the van and walk to where the tour began.

It was an excellent tour, and they saw everything they wanted to see. They even had time to stop in Golden Gate Park for a bathroom break. There was one other stop and that was towards the end of the tour. The guide had saved Chinatown for last.

That made all of them happy. Tony asked the guide, who was giving them a short walking excursion of the area, if they could leave the tour early after he was finished speaking. He had no problem with them ending there. The guide pointed out some good restaurants in that part of the city and showed Tony where to go to get the cable car back to the wharf.

Giving the man a nice tip they all started walking towards a restaurant they thought sounded good. After lunch they had no trouble getting the cable car for the ride back down to the wharf. They had saved time not having to go back and forth to Chinatown so they did not have to hurry for their boat ride.

It was a typical San Francisco summer day. The sun was shining, which was not always a given, but it was very cool. That was normal at this time of the year. They were just happy there was no fog. The temperatures inland often reached the high 90s. That combined with the cool air coming off the Pacific Ocean created the cool weather and also the fog.

People are often surprised by how cool the temperatures are in the summer in San Francisco. Because of this fact the street vendors sell sweatshirts for $12.00. Everyone decided to buy one since the price was so cheap, and they had only brought light jackets. They knew the sweatshirts would come in handy especially on the bay cruise.

At a few minutes before 3:00 p.m. they were in line for their boat cruise. They were all given headsets that explained everything they were seeing, especially the buildings on the shoreline. They were so glad Tony had suggested the boat ride since they saw the city from a whole different perspective. Going under the Golden Gate Bridge and around Alcatraz Island really added to the adventure.

From there they walked to Pier 39 and shopped a little, took pictures of the sea lions and had a nice seafood dinner as they watched the sun setting. Tony realized that Julia and Henry were getting tired and suggested everyone wait for him on the sidewalk in front of the pier.

As the men walked to get the van, Hugh mentioned how compatible Julia and Henry were. "I noticed they are constantly holding hands and often finish each other's sentences. I know they have been married a long time, but they seem so happy to be with each other. I wish we could have been lucky enough to have marriages like that."

"You're right, Hugh. They prove it is possible to have a happy marriage. However, after what we have been through, I am not willing to give it another go. Are you?"

"Definitely not!"

It was not long before the men picked up the other four waiting on the street for them. As they drove over the Bay Bridge, they looked to the left and saw the Wharf area. It had been a fun day and they had seen so many things. They were sorry they had so little time in that place.

Tomorrow they would be driving down to Monterey and Carmel. It would be a much more leisurely day and give them time to relax before their final day in this region. Everyone slept well that night, and it was not long before they were on their way south of the city the next day.

Riley sat up front with Tony with a map on her lap. She also had a guide book and pointed out some of the sites along the way. They decided to go to Carmel-By-The-Sea first since it was the farthest away. Along the two hour journey they saw some typical California trees, the kind one saw in the movies that were characteristic of the Pacific Coast.

Carmel was a very small village with quaint shops and several B & B's. One had been owned by Clint Eastwood and he had even been mayor for a time. Doris Day was another famous resident of that town and had a shelter for rescued animals. The town was exceptionally dog friendly. On the Monterey Peninsula, Carmel was known for its natural scenery and rich artistic history.

The downtown was only about four blocks long. They strolled through the shops, many with an artistic flair, and found a little café to have lunch. They pushed two outside tables together, and found dogs with their owners at all the other tables.

Riley, who had been studying the guide book on their drive said, "Do you know they even passed a law that made it illegal to wear high heels in town? As you have seen the streets are pretty uneven and I guess they did not want to get sued."

"Well whatever the laws are here, this is one of the prettiest little seaside towns I have seen along our coastal journey and I am glad we came," Phoebe added.

After lunch they took the famous 17 mile drive to Monterey. Hugh mentioned how weird it was to have to pay to drive the road, since you can see the beautiful ocean vistas everywhere else for free.

On the way Riley once again told them what she had read. "The city had California's first theater, public building, public library, publicly funded school, printing press, and newspaper. The area has attracted artists since the late 19th century, and many celebrated painters and writers lived here."

Then she continued, "You are probably aware that John Steinbeck lived in the city, and immortalized Monterey in his novels *Cannery Row*, *Tortilla Flat*, and *East of Eden*.

Until the 1950s there was an abundant fishery. Some of the famous attractions today are the Monterey Bay Aquarium, Fisherman's Wharf and the annual Monterey Jazz Festival. But right now we are headed for Cannery Row. There are a lot of restaurants and cute shops, and after we spend some time there we may want to check out the Aquarium, since it is so famous."

They had a wonderful afternoon and a light dinner just south of San Jose. They thought the stop would help to ease some of the bad rush hour traffic before they continued on to Oakland. The traffic was a little slow in some areas, but much lighter than if they had not stopped for dinner. They had taken the interstate and had avoided San Francisco traffic which was a plus. They arrived at the Pullman by 8:00 p.m., and although tired, they all were happy about their wonderful adventure.

The next day they planned to cross the Golden Gate Bridge to Muir Woods and follow the coast north for a while. Julia and Henry decided to spend the day on the Pullman resting, as they knew they would be doing a lot of driving for the next few days. They thought a day of relaxing would be nice, especially since they had already been north of the city. There was a café close to the train station they planned to go to for lunch.

Since neither of the women had ever been in this part of the country, they loved going over the Golden Gate Bridge and were astounded with Muir Woods. As they walked through the grove of Redwoods over one hundred feet tall, they marveled at the old growth forest.

Riley reminded everyone what the guide in Yosemite had told them about redwood trees. "Those in the Sierra

Nevada were the giant sequoias. They are slightly shorter but more massive than these trees. The trees here and those we will see going through 'The Avenue of the Giants' are called Coast Redwoods. These trees grow in the moist climate of this area with winter rains and summer fog. They keep so much water in their trunks that even a fire won't burn them down."

As they walked along the paths they were in awe of these giant trees that almost totally blocked the sky and sun. Luckily it was a dry day which made it more fun for walking around.

When they left Muir Woods, they went north on the cliff road of Highway 1. At times it was a challenging highway, but the views along the ocean were well worth seeing. They stopped for lunch at a little seaside restaurant before heading inland and south again.

Tony and Riley both thought they should take Highway 101 to Oakland to avoid San Francisco traffic on the way back. 101 was also the road they were taking out of town the next day. They found themselves back at the Pullman by 5:00 p.m.

At breakfast they had asked Margaret if they could have an earlier dinner. They would then have time to pack their clothes since they would be departing the train in the morning for several days. The Pullman would be coupled onto the Coast Starlight for its trip to Portland, Oregon where they would meet up with it again.

At 6:00 p.m. they sat down to another excellent dinner. Once again Charles served his Brandy Alexander's for dessert. Margaret had spent the day, with Charles' help, getting the dirty laundry washed.

After finishing their after dinner drink everyone departed for their rooms. Once in their rooms they sorted through their clean clothes and packed what they needed for their trip up the coast. As they went to sleep they all were thinking of the amazing time they had in the San Francisco area.

Chapter 17

Sadly they said goodbye to "The City by the Bay" the next morning and headed north on Highway 101. They stopped at a winery in Napa Valley. Tony did not sample anything since he was driving. They bought a couple of bottles so they could have a drink in the evenings when they settled into their hotels.

Once again they stopped at a grocery store and bought food to make a picnic lunch. Their first attraction as they headed north were the California State Parks where they saw many redwood groves as they drove the thirty-two mile "Avenue of the Giants." They made two stops. The first was the Humboldt Interpretive and Welcome Center where Charles Kellogg's "Travel Log" was on display.

Kellogg was a vaudeville performer who imitated bird songs. He later campaigned for the protection of the California redwood forests. He constructed a mobile home, called the "Travel Log", out of a redwood tree, and drove it around the country to raise awareness of the plight of the California forests. Its maximum speed was 18 mph. Looking at it you could just picture the man driving the log.

Henry and Julia sat on a Redwood bench as the other four went across the street to walk through a grove of trees. Hugh lead the way followed by Phoebe then Riley with Tony at the rear.

It was awe inspiring looking up at the trees that soared overhead. There was not much light since the trees made a canopy above them that blocked the sun. All of a sudden Tony saw Riley starting to trip over a large root coming out of the ground.

Since he had been walking close behind, he was able to grab her around the waist. Her hand automatically clutched his, as she righted herself. From out of nowhere she felt a tingling go through her body, as she touched Tony's hand. She quickly removed her hand from the back of his.

Wow, what just happened she thought to herself, as she regained her balance. She did not realize Tony had also felt a slight shock when her hand touched his. Although neither said anything to each other about what had occurred, they were both surprised by what had just happened.

All she could mumble was "Thanks, Tony," as she quickly moved to catch up with Phoebe. As they exited the grove of trees, to go back to the welcome center where their van was parked, neither looked at the other.

The first town after the "Avenue of the Giants" was Eureka. This was an old lumbering town. They drove through a residential area that contained some beautiful Victorian homes which had been lovingly restored.

They discovered that the nicer hotels had been booked by several tour buses. So they decided to push on to

Crescent City located very close to the Oregon border. A great deal of the town had been destroyed by a tsunami in 1964. Over half the waterfront business district, consisting of thirty blocks, had been decimated by waves twenty to twenty-one feet high. This had happened when Alaska had a 9.2 earthquake which spawned a tsunami that was felt up and down the California coast.

They checked in to a nice motel overlooking the Pacific Ocean that had breakfast included. The owner suggested a local seafood restaurant and they were not disappointed. Being on the coast none of them could get enough fresh seafood. They had a long driving day, but the pace would be slower now that they were close to the Oregon border.

Everyone was looking forward to the Oregon coast. The two ladies and Hugh had never been there before. Tony had talked a lot about the beauty of the area and they were all excited that they were headed for there.

The dinner conversation was light and happy. As Riley was making a comment to Tony, she realized things were back to normal. It was almost as if the touch, and her reaction to it, had not happened. She had no idea Tony was thinking the same thing.

It had almost been like a school girl's reaction to a boy in her classroom. She was still a little shocked that she had reacted to his touch. She had loved her husband dearly but the excitement they felt with each other when they first met had been gone for years.

Their relationship had evolved into being comfortable with each other much like Henry and Julia. She did not think it was possible to feel that kind of sexual excitement towards another man again. So she convinced herself that it had just been in her imagination.

Tony also felt he had imagined it. As he often told Hugh, marriage for him had been as painful as walking around with a rock in his shoe. He did not want a serious relationship with anyone. It was as though there was a fence around him, and he was not going to let anyone break it.

He realized he liked Riley a lot. The way she had taken her duties so seriously, even to map reading, was something he admired. Since she had a long happy marriage, he knew she was probably very easy to get along with. However he was definitely not interested in anything long term. He hoped when they finished this journey they could still be friends and date casually. Otherwise he would make it a point to never see her again.

After dinner they returned to their motel. Riley never said anything to Phoebe about what had happened. Since she had no intention of pursuing a serious relationship with anyone, including Tony, she thought the best thing was to forget that anything happened.

Chapter 18

They had decided to leave at 8:00 a.m. the next day. Everyone was in the breakfast room by 7:00 a.m. They all loved the fact that everyone was punctual. They knew they were on vacation but they had two attractions they planned for the day, if they could fit them in. Because of this, they wanted to get an early start. Their first stop was Gold Beach where the Rogue River emptied into the ocean.

Hugh had checked online and found there was a jet boat ride that began at 10:00 a.m. They decided that would be fun, since they would also learn about the local geography and history. When they got to the parking lot, they saw two gift shops.

Phoebe had joked previously that there must be a law that no attraction in the United States could exist without a gift shop. Although they knew she wasn't serious about it being a law, they all agreed with her assessment.

It was cold and windy when they went down the steps to get into the boat. It was a large boat that held over fifty passengers. There were about twenty people besides themselves going on the two hour journey that averaged about twenty-five miles. Julia and Henry were not sure about doing the boat ride, but the others talked them into coming along.

They were very glad they decided to go. As soon as they rounded the curve that put them from the ocean to the river the water became very calm. The wind also let up and the further inland they went the warmer the temperature became. They all took their sweaters off after they got underway.

It was very peaceful on the river. Sometimes the boat went very fast and other times very slow, as they travelled through the spectacular Hellgate Canyon Wilderness Area. They saw eagles and sandhill cranes while the guide told them about the landscape and history of the place.

When they returned from the exhilarating ride they had lunch at a seafood restaurant that was located right in the marina called the Port Hole Cafe. They thought they probably could not go wrong with a name like that. After lunch they continued up the coast to Florence. All afternoon there were awesome views of the Pacific Coast as they drove.

They traveled on a narrow winding road and they were able to see the ocean pounding against the coastline. They saw spectacular monolith rocks close to the shore with waves crashing against them. They made a stop at a lighthouse where they could see large kelp beds floating in the water. They could also hear sea lions barking that they knew lived in caves along the coast.

The road they were driving was three hundred sixty three miles long from Brookings to Astoria. As they drove, the scenery constantly changed. Sometimes they saw marshy areas. Other times it was agricultural valleys. And often wind sculpted dunes. They drove through several pretty seaside towns, but the highlight was always the view of the ocean with the rolling waves hitting the shore.

They decided to stay overnight in Florence and found a hotel right on the beach. After Henry and Julia were settled in, the other four took off for a dune buggy ride along the ocean at the Oregon Dunes National Recreation Area. This area was like a forty seven mile sandbox.

The dune buggies held twenty-four people with a ten person minimum. They had called in for a reservation when they knew they would make it on time. The owner had told them eight other people had wanted to go and with the four of them the tour would definitely go. It was a one hour narrated tour that covered eight miles of dunes and two miles of beach.

They had put on their sweatshirts from San Francisco and brought their jackets. They were glad they dressed so warmly. The ride was a lot of fun, but it was chilly. When they went into the wind near the beach they felt like their faces were getting sandblasted. But, like the jet boat, this was another ride they would not have missed for the world.

They returned to the hotel, took showers, and with Henry and Julia in tow got in the van and headed to the old town. The hotel manager had told them about a very reasonable and picturesque restaurant that served fresh seafood. Once again they were glad they had asked.

They talked about taking a walk on the beach, since there would still be another hour of daylight after dinner. They had spent a lot of time sitting during the day, and thought it would not only be great exercise but also a refreshing thing to do.

Hugh however decided not to go. His friend, who owned the mansion for the foster children, was having some issues and needed his advice. Since it was better to reach the man at night, Hugh thought it was important to take the time to call him. Henry and Julia also declined the walk.

That left Tony and the two women. As they headed towards the beach, Phoebe's cell phone rang. They stopped and looked at her when she answered. After listening for a few seconds she looked at them and said, "I have to take this call. It is my daughter and I haven't spoken to her for a couple of days. I am going back to my room. You two might as well go on without me."

Riley was not sure what to do. If she decided to skip the walk and go back to her room, it might look like something was wrong. Besides it was just a walk on the beach. She decided to pretend there was nothing weird about walking alone with Tony. Looking at him she said, "I guess it is just the two of us."

He just nodded as he turned to walk down by the water.

The waves were rolling in and the wind was blowing, but it did not feel really cold. The noise of the waves however was so loud they could not talk to each other. Riley was definitely pleased about that.

Ever since they had started their walk her stomach was doing flip flops. She kept looking out to sea, as she walked, worried Tony would notice something in her demeanor.

She was afraid to look at him in case he realized what she was thinking even though she knew that was ridiculous.

Tony was having issues of his own. His stomach was also doing flip flops, and he did not understand it. Why am I feeling this way he thought? I don't really know this woman. I have been dating off and on for years and have never felt this excitement about someone in the past.

As he was thinking about the situation, he did not realize he was frowning until he looked up and saw Riley, who had stopped walking stare at him.

"What's wrong?"

"Are you all right? You have such a frown on your face I thought perhaps you were in some kind of pain."

"No, I am fine. I guess I was just thinking about something that was not too pleasant. We have been walking over twenty minutes. Maybe we should turn around and go back. I don't want to be out here when it gets dark."

"That is fine with me," Riley said with a sigh of relief. Luckily he did not hear her sigh over the waves.

The two of them did not speak on the return. As they walked down the hallway of their hotel they nodded at each other and entered their rooms quickly closing their doors.

This is turning into something I can't seem to control Riley was thinking. Even though it had been almost an hour, Phoebe was sitting on her bed still talking to her daughter when she entered the room. She did not notice that her friend was troubled, as she headed to the bathroom.

I know he is feeling something. Neither one of us is acting friendly and nonchalant like we did before. There is a definite current in the air when we are together. I just don't know what to do to get things back to normal. It seems as though I have a constant stomach ache when I am around him.

I have to start pretending this is not happening. If I don't, everyone is going to quickly sense something is going on. With that she put on her nightgown, washed her face and brushed her teeth. When she came out of the bathroom she gave a quick wave to Phoebe and climbed into bed facing away from her friend.

Hugh was still on the phone when Tony entered the room. He also headed to the bathroom and went straight to bed when he came out. He desperately wanted things to go back to the way they were previously between him and Riley. He knew Hugh would be shocked by what he was feeling.

Both Riley and Tony had a very troubled sleep that night. They tossed and turned and kept wondering how they could change things back to the way they used to be.

Chapter 19

Neither one of them needed to worry the next day. Hugh had eaten something that had upset his stomach the evening before, and he had gotten up very sick in the middle of the night. They were planning on driving the rest of the coast to Astoria before heading to Portland.

Astoria was where Lewis and Clark spent the winter on their trek west. Since Hugh insisted they keep moving they decided to skip Astoria and instead turn east at Tillamook, famous for having the largest cheese factory in Oregon. The factory has been giving tours to tourists for over one hundred years. They had about a two hour drive to Tillamook and a little over two and a half on an inland road to Portland.

They waited until 10:00 a.m.to leave to give Hugh more time to rest before they got on the road. He had taken some medicine to keep from being sick while they were traveling. Hopefully leaving a little later would give the pills time to start working.

Hugh fell back asleep after taking the medicine. So Phoebe, Riley, and Tony took a walk on the beach after breakfast. They were talking about their change of plans when Riley realized she and Tony seemed back to normal. Halleluiah she thought. Maybe things will just continue as they were when we started this trip.

Phoebe called Charles to let him know they would be getting to Portland early. The Pullman had arrived the night before, so they knew it would be there waiting for them.

Since the front passenger seat reclined quite a bit they put Hugh up there, so he could rest more comfortably. Riley climbed into the middle seat with Phoebe. They stopped in Tillamook to use the bathroom and took the self guided factory tour. Hugh stayed in the van resting. When the tour was over they ate some cheese and had sandwiches before their trip to Portland. It was just after 3:00 p.m. when they arrived at the train station.

They were all happy to be back "home" and glad they had missed rush hour. They still had the van for two more days, as they planned to stay in the area that long. Charles met them at the station and showed Tony where to park the van. Once again he had to take them by golf cart to the Pullman.

Phoebe went with Julia, Henry and Hugh on the first run. Hugh had felt better for hours, but had nothing to eat or drink and still felt very weak. Charles was planning on bringing the suitcases on the second run but Phoebe had grabbed Hugh's before they left the station.

As Charles went back to get the others, Phoebe unpacked Hugh's bag finding his pajamas. She went to put some of her things in her bedroom, as he took a shower. He was just climbing into bed when she returned with some ginger ale. She knew he needed to keep some liquids down, or he would get dehydrated.

He was so thirsty he drank the whole glassful. That she took as a good sign. As she put the blankets over him, she heard him mumble "thanks." But she realized he was asleep before she finished tucking him in. She took his glass and returned with another one full of ice water. She placed the glass on his nightstand in case he woke up needing a drink.

The five of them had an early dinner and then Julia and Henry went to their room to unpack and rest. The other three went up to the dome car to discuss their itinerary.

"I think we need to keep things as planned. I know Hugh came to Seattle a couple of years ago and went to Mount St. Helens. So if he is not up to it tomorrow, he can skip going with us. But he has never been to Portland and is looking forward to our trip along the Columbia River Gorge."

"I think you are right, Tony. I have been looking at the maps and we will drive a ways to the volcano, as well as, making a few stops. I do not want to be rushed and worried about making it back to Portland in time, since the train leaves at 4:00 p.m. in the afternoon."

Phoebe added, "I agree with both of you. Tomorrow we will do Mount St. Helens and the next day the Columbia River Gorge. That way we will be back in plenty of time to continue on to Seattle."

After agreeing to keep things as they stood, Phoebe went to her room to unpack. Tony asked Riley if he could talk to her for a few minutes. Riley agreed while hoping he was not going to say anything personal to her.

"I know you want to go to your room and unpack, but I really wanted to go over our routes for the next two days. With these narrow mountain roads I do not want to miss a turn or go down a road I don't really want because the GPS sends me there. I am mostly concerned with the Columbia River Gorge region."

"I know tomorrow is a long day, Tony. I would much rather do this tonight, so we don't have to do it tomorrow night. Thanks for asking for the help now."

"That's great. I know we all wanted to go up to Mount Hood to the Timberline Lodge, and I found some back roads to take us back to Portland. Timing will be tight that day. The train leaves for Seattle in the late afternoon and we do not want to miss it. Luckily, I was able to talk the rental car place into picking up the van at the station as they did in Grand Junction. So we won't have to worry about that."

Riley and Tony spent about a half an hour going over the maps. Riley decided to use a highlighter so she could stay on track more easily. When they finished up they both felt a sense of accomplishment.

After that, Riley went off to her bedroom to unpack. Tony was not tired and did not want to disturb Hugh. Because of that he went to the parlor to read. He had not thought about it earlier since everything had been in such a state of flux, but he now realized he and Riley were back to being completely normal around each other again.

Maybe he had imagined his new feelings towards her. They had never said anything to each other. Well whatever, he thought. I am just glad we are back to where we used to be.

He only read for a little while and turned in early. It only took him five minutes to unpack. Most of the clothes in his suitcase were dirty, so he put those in the laundry bag for Margaret. He was tired after sleeping so badly the night before, and they had agreed they wanted to be on the road the next morning by 8:00 a.m.

Chapter 20

The sun was shining as they were eating breakfast the next morning. The weatherman was calling for highs in the 70's. It would be a perfect day for their trip to the volcano.

Hugh had gotten up when the others did, but still felt weak. He had awakened once in the middle of the night to use the bathroom, and drink the glass of water Phoebe had left. He agreed with Tony that he should skip going to Mount St. Helens. He sat with them while they ate and had some tea and toast. It tasted good, but he was ready to sleep again when they departed.

Since there were no suitcases, Charles was able to get everyone into the golf cart for one run to the station where the van was parked. Hugh waved good-bye to everyone as they left in the golf cart and went back to bed. As they climbed into the van, they realized that luckily they would be headed in the opposite direction of the rush hour traffic.

The Willamette River in Portland is the dividing point between the Oregon and Washington borders. It did not take them long to get to the state of Washington. They took Interstate 5 north to the exit for the mountain.

Not long after entering the state they exited the interstate and drove five miles east to the Silver Lake Visitor Center. It was hard to believe that it was over thirty five years since the volcano erupted. In 1982 President Ronald Reagan had named the region a National Monument. It is managed by the U.S. Forest Service.

The Mount St. Helens Visitor Center at Silver Lake opened in 1987, and is maintained by the Washington State Park System. The exhibits they saw included the area's culture and history, as well as the natural history and geology of the volcano, and its eruption. The Center had a gift shop, naturally. But there was also a theater with an excellent overview film of the eruption and the way the place looked afterwards.

In the three years after the centered opened over one and a half million people stopped there on the way up the mountain. It was a very popular place. When they arrived there, a tour bus was already in the parking lot.

After stopping at the Visitor Center they began driving the over fifty miles to The Johnston Ridge Observatory which is at the end of the road up the mountain. The exhibits there focus on the geologic history of the volcano, eyewitness accounts of the explosion, and the science of monitoring volcanic activity. There were ranger-led programs available every hour, as well as, a half-mile trail with views of the lava dome, crater, pumice plain, and landslide deposit.

There was also a movie that was totally awesome. It told the story of the eruption on a big screen with curtains on each side. When the movie was over the screen was raised up and the curtains opened to big picture windows. And right in their line of sight was the volcano. Phoebe knew she would never forget the surprised reaction she felt, nor the gasps she heard around the room as the volcano was revealed in front of them.

They sat outside at picnic tables looking at the mountain while they had lunch. After they finished eating they followed a ranger who did a talk along the trail. It was a really beautiful day. They knew how fortunate they were when they overheard some people from California talking. This was their second visit this year. The last time they had come the mountain had been totally obscured by clouds, and they could not see a thing.

"I guess we were really lucky," Phoebe said as they made their way back down the mountain. They ran into a little rush hour traffic on the way back into Portland. It was not as bad as the traffic coming out of the city, however. The day was still clear and they could see Mount Hood, where they were going tomorrow, off to their left.

Portland's population is over 620,000 so they were not surprised to run into traffic. What did surprise them was how little traffic there was in the city center. Portland had free light rail downtown, and it was obviously well used. It was 5:30 p.m. when they pulled into the train station.

Phoebe had called Charles and he was waiting with the golf cart when they arrived. Tony quickly parked the van in the space allotted them, and before they knew it they were back at the Pullman. Hugh was waiting for them and looked a lot better. He told them he had slept most of the day and when he woke up after 4:00 p.m., he knew he we going to live again.

At dinner they told him about their day, and since he had been there recently he could picture everything they had done. While they were eating he felt well enough to tell them about the city since he had been assigned that duty.

"Portland was named after the city in Maine and settled in the 1830s near the end of the Oregon Trail. The river provided convenient transportation of goods, and the timber industry was a major force in the city's early economy."

Then he continued. "Portland actually has two nicknames. There are many bridges across the river downtown, several of which are historical landmarks, and so the city has been called 'Bridgetown' for a long time. The International Rose Test Garden is also here which I know you are aware. There are over 7,000 rose plants of approximately 550 varieties. The roses bloom from April through October but the peak is in June. Tony and I thought we should make a quick stop there tomorrow on our way out of town."

"And that is why the other nickname is the "City of Roses," Aunt Julia chimed in.

Everyone looked at her with a smile when she said that.

"Well, I for one am going to call it an early night," Hugh added. "Tony and I think we should leave by 7:30 a.m. I know that is early but we want to stop at the park to see the roses before the Columbia River Gorge ride. Since the train leaves in the late afternoon, we definitely do not want to miss it. It is hard to believe we will be in Seattle tomorrow night."

Agreeing with Hugh, everyone went to their rooms after dessert. Even Tony decided to read in his room instead of the parlor. He thought he would get sleepier that way.

Chapter 21

True to their word they were in the van by 7:45 a.m. headed to the Rose Garden and just after 8:30 a.m. they were headed out of town. The Columbia River, on their left, was the last river Lewis and Clark journeyed on to get to the Pacific coast.

At breakfast that morning Tony had told everyone about their journey. "The Columbia River Gorge is a canyon up to 4,000 feet deep that stretches over eighty miles, although we won't travel that far. It winds through the Cascade Mountain range and while we will be in Oregon you will see the state of Washington on the other side."

As they listened he continued, "This was the first scenic highway to be given National Historic Landmark designation. It was considered a great engineering feat designed in 1913-14 to take advantage of the waterfalls and other beautiful spots. Built as a comfort station on the old highway our first stop will be the historic Vista House."

As they drove, just as Tony had told them, the road completely circled around the Vista House. And just as the name implied, they had terrific views of the river gorge area. Some of the cliffs were over 2,000 feet high and they stopped to take pictures before continuing on to the Falls.

Multnomah Falls is the tallest waterfall in the state of Oregon and the second tallest in the U.S. The falls drop in two major steps, split into an upper falls of 542 feet and a lower falls of 69 feet. The top portion of the falls could be seen from the highway, but you had to walk up a steep walkway to see the bottom portion. There was an even steeper path to the top of the lower falls which they all did in order to take pictures.

They were lucky, since it was so early in the morning they did not have to park too far away or fight hoards of people. According to Native American legend the Falls were created to win the heart of a young princess who wanted a hidden place to bathe. Naturally they thought they should see as much as possible while there.

"I'll bet this place is a mad house on weekends," Riley observed.

Agreeing with her, after their hike and a bathroom stop, they got back in the van and continued on. They drove past the Bonneville Dam next. They knew they could visit that place, but had all agreed they wanted to go to Mount Hood. They were worried the dam would take too much time.

Just past the Hood River they took a county road south through the lava beds at Parkdale to Mount Hood, 11,239 feet tall. This was the mountain they had seen in the distance on their way back home the previous day. They were headed to Timberline Lodge for lunch.

Riley had bought a book in Yosemite called "The Great

Lodges of the West" and wanted to see as many as possible. She had read that Timberline Lodge was built in the late 1930s, by the Works Progress Administration. The workers used large timbers and local stone, and placed intricately carved decorative elements throughout the building. It was listed as a National Historic Landmark and sits at an elevation of 5,960 feet. There are over a million visitors annually, many of whom come to ski.

They had a very nice lunch. Phoebe also bought a copy of the Great Lodges book in the bookstore before they left. Then they followed a two lane state road sixty miles back to Portland.

They arrived at 2:30 p.m. Once again Tony left the keys to the van in an envelope with the station master, so the rental agency could pick it up. It took Charles two runs in the golf cart to get everyone to the Pullman. However, on the second trip a worker at the station came along so she could take the cart back to where it belonged when everyone was on the train.

Their car had already been taken to a different track from where they had spent the last two nights. It was all ready for the 4:00 p.m. departure. When the Amtrak train arrived it just needed to back up and couple the Pullman. They were all excited to be moving again. This was a very short trip, since it was only 4 hours to Seattle.

They knew they would enjoy the ride. Since they were so far north, they realized it would be light the whole distance. They would be following the Cascade Mountains along the I-5 interstate. To the east they would go by Mount Hood, Mount St, Helens, and Mount Rainier. They were not sure, if they would see Mount Adams, near Yakima, that sat a little behind Mount Rainier. They knew they probably would not see Mount Baker. That was up near the border of Canada on I-5 and the last of the volcanic mountains in this range.

In no time at all they were underway. They not only had dinner in the dome car but sat up there all the way, to Seattle so they could better take in the views.

Chapter 22

It was 8:00 p.m. when they arrived in Seattle. They did not get off the train that evening. Instead they stayed with the Pullman after it was parked. Tony had called the rental car agency to make sure the van had been delivered. They assured him it had. The car was parked in a lot next to the station, and the keys were in the station manager's office.

They had packed for an overnight off the train and were up early the next morning. They were on their way to Mount Rainier. After returning from the mountain they would take the road near Tacoma that would take them to the Olympic Peninsula and Port Angeles for their overnight stay. Then the next day they would take the ferry to Victoria, BC. They would definitely be going at a fast pace the next two days.

They knew they did not have enough time to explore the peninsula the way they wanted to. Because of that fact, they were chatting in the van about all the places they needed to come back to on another trip. Phoebe smiled to herself when she heard everyone discussing another trip as though it were a given. Truth be told she realized she would love to do more trips with everyone, too.

They were on the road by 7:15 a.m. They drove south towards Tacoma. Not only was "the mountain out" but the heavier traffic was headed in the opposite direction. Seeing the mountain was a spectacular sight that was not always a given. Often the clouds obscured the top half. As he was driving Tony started telling everyone what he had read about their destination.

"At 14,410 feet Mount Rainier is a symbol of the Seattle landscape and the highest mountain in the Cascade Range. John Muir climbed the mountain in 1888 and although he enjoyed the view, he conceded that it was best appreciated from below. Then in 1899, President William McKinley established the area as America's fifth National Park."

As they were looking upward he continued, "This mountain is an active volcano with two craters and several glaciers. Even though there is no evidence of an imminent eruption, if it did erupt as powerfully as Mount St. Helens, the effect would be much greater. That is because of the far more massive amounts of glacial ice on the volcano and the more heavily populated areas surrounding it."

They continued towards the Nisqually entrance. As they entered they soon discovered that the park roads were winding with narrow shoulders and a maximum speed limit of 35 mph. They made their way towards Paradise as the tall Western Red Cedar trees loomed overhead and in some areas totally blocked the sky above them.

They made a couple of picture stops and arrived at Paradise about 11:00 a.m. They were at 5400 feet in elevation and surrounded by wildflower meadows. This was a busy place. In the summer people came for hiking and mountain climbing. But winter sports were also popular since the mountain received over 640 inches of snow annually. As they walked along the path to the lodge, it was hard to imagine the area got that much snow since presently there was grass and flowers surrounding them.

They had seen pictures in their book on lodges, but as they walked into the building they realized the pictures did not do justice as seeing the building in person. They checked out the gift shop, book store, and also looked into the dining room. They decided to go over to the Visitor Center, since there was a movie and a cafeteria in that building.

After the movie and lunch they walked partly up the mountain on a trail that had been recommended by a ranger. Although the top of the mountain was filled with glaciers, they were walking in a large meadow filled with beautiful multi-colored wildflowers. It was only in the high 50s, but the sun felt very warm.

They spent about a half hour walking. When they left Paradise they made a stop at the first pullover they came to. Julia and Henry stood at the top, as the other four made their way down a steep path beside a waterfall. The ranger had told them about this stop, and they were so glad they had found it. As the path wound around they got to the end, and there they could see the bottom of the waterfall with a beautiful double rainbow arced across. It was a sight they knew they would always remember.

They stopped at Longmire, the original park's headquarters and a designated National Historic district, before exiting. They were headed towards Tacoma, and the road that would take them over to the Olympic Peninsula.

As they crossed the Tacoma Narrows Bridge once again Riley told them what the guide book said. "This is the fifth largest suspension span in the world, and the water below us is part of Puget Sound. This bridge was completed in 1940 and became known as 'Galloping Gertie' when it collapsed in a wind storm four months later. It was 'the most dramatic failure in bridge engineering history.' The sunken remains were placed on the National Registry of Historic Places in 1992 to protect the bridge remains from scavengers."

As they were driving across the bridge she continued, "It took twenty-nine months to build this new safer bridge which opened in 1950. It was designed to carry 60,000 cars a day but averages over 90,000 vehicles daily."

They knew it was silly, but they were all happy when they reached the other side. As they continued along they passed a cute little town called Port Gamble. "It would be nice to spend some time there," Hugh noted.

"I cannot tell you how much we are missing along this route," Julia added. "I know we have limited time and are just hitting the highlights but we could easily spend two to three days on this peninsula."

As they crossed over the Hood Canal Bridge, the longest floating bridge in the United States, Riley pointed out another road. That highway would take them to Bainbridge Island and the ferry back to Seattle on their return. There was a sign for Port Townsend, and Julia mentioned what a cute town that was. After passing that area, there were many signs for lavender farms, and a town called Sequim where John Wayne once kept a boat.

As they continued driving, the mountains of the Olympic National Park lay ahead. With all the Western Red Cedar trees looming around them it seemed to be a very brooding area.

Hugh, who had been to the peninsula previously said, "Look at that tall mountain over to our left. That is Mount Olympus, at almost 8,000 feet, and the tallest mountain in the park. The park covers much of the peninsula and the park headquarters are right in Port Angeles where we are headed. It is too bad we do not have the time since it will be evening when we arrive. Otherwise we could take the road that goes up to the top called Hurricane Ridge. It is an awesome sight, as you can imagine. But they close the road at night, because it is too dangerous to drive in the dark."

"The waterfalls and glacier lakes in the park are also a sight to behold. There are herds of Roosevelt elk you can often spot in the meadows. As you get closer to the ocean, the countryside becomes a rainforest. FDR created the park and it has been named a World Heritage site because of its exceptional beauty," Julia added.

"I guess this is another place we have to add to our return bucket list," Phoebe said smiling.

It was 7:30 p.m. when they arrived at their hotel, the Red Lion. It was the only hotel in Port Angeles on the water. They had requested the premium waterfront views, and when they checked into their hotel their request had been granted. Their rooms were right next to each other, and they all had little patios. As they looked outside the Strait of Juan de Fuca lay stretched in front of them.

Because it was late they had dinner in the hotel dining

room. The restaurant had large picture windows, and as they ate they watched the sun set. The colors were incredible as darkness descended. They had a long day, but it had been very enjoyable. However, there was another long day facing them tomorrow, so they went to their rooms as soon as they finished eating.

Chapter 23

It was 6:40 a.m. when they got in line for the ferry. The *MV Coho* was anchored directly in front of them. The boat left at 7:30 a.m., and they needed to clear Customs and Immigration first. It was early but a beautiful morning with the sun shining. They were hoping it would be a nice day, rather than foggy, for the ninety minute crossing.

They had not eaten breakfast at the hotel. They knew there was a cafeteria on board the ship and after they got their food they settled at a table with windows looking out at the Strait. This was another journey Julia and Henry had done previously. But it was a new adventure for the other four.

When they arrived in Victoria Tony drove the van off the boat, and once again they went through customs. They knew the city was internationally renowned as the "City of Gardens." They saw well over a thousand hanging baskets on the lampposts all over the downtown and inner harbor area.

It was a half hour drive to their first destination, Butchart Gardens. On the way Hugh told them the history of the gardens which contained over seven hundred varieties of

1,000,000 bedding plants. There would definitely be a lot of walking ahead of them

"Robert Butchart and his wife Jenny, who were from Ontario, went to England on their honeymoon. While there he learned an important process for manufacturing Portland cement which involved using sacks instead of barrels and special kilns to burn limestone. In 1904 he started a plant near Victoria. While he was busy with his cement, Jenny got busy with her flowers. Between their house and the ocean she developed the Japanese Garden. It was so beautiful that her husband supplied some men from his plant to help her."

They were all nodding as he continued. "When the limestone quarry was depleted, Jenny started the sunken gardens. The men hung ropes for her so she could get up and down the sides of the quarry to plant her creeping vines and flowers. She had tons of soil brought in and trees from all over the world. By the 1930s, thousands had visited her gardens."

"You haven't even mentioned her rose garden. There are paths and pullovers where you can sit and look at the flowers throughout the area," Henry added. "We visited here about twenty years ago after I retired and it inspired me to start my own garden. Nothing on a scale as grand as this one though," he said smiling.

"As long as I have your attention let me tell you a little about Victoria," Hugh chimed in. We just crossed the Strait of Juan de Fuca as you are aware. We are now on Vancouver Island. On the other side of the island is The Strait of Georgia. On the mainland across that strait is the city of Vancouver. The island is 252 miles long, but on the Pacific Ocean side there are only roads about half way up. The area was settled in the 1840s, but the Fraser Valley Gold Rush in 1858 helped the area grow as a major port of entry."

Hugh continued, "In 1862 the first of the Bride Ships arrived. The men who were looking for a wife would stand on a soapbox or high rock extolling their merits. If the woman decided to wed, the marriage took place immediately. The gold rush was also a springboard for the arrival of several thousand Chinese immigrants who came to work on the construction of the Canadian Pacific Railway in the 1880s. Today the city has a very strong economy due to Canada's western naval base located here, as well as a major fishing fleet, technology, and, of course, tourism."

Sitting next to him in the van Phoebe added, "I am looking forward to high tea this afternoon at the Empress Hotel. I read they serve 500,000 cups of tea a year. With all the walking we will be doing this morning I can eat whatever I like."

They all laughed while agreeing with her statement.

It felt like they walked forever in the gardens. On the way back to the inner harbor they drove through neighborhoods that had large mansions facing the sea with small bungalow cottages interspersed. They drove through China Town and saw Fan Tan Alley, one of the narrowest streets in the world made famous by the Goldie Hawn/ Mel Gibson movie, *Bird On A Wire*.

They found a place to park near the ferry office and walked by the beautiful Parliament building on their way to Thunderbird Park. The park was behind the Empress hotel near the Royal British Columbia Museum. It contained a collection of replica Totem Poles from the time of the first contact between the colonists and the First Nations (as the Indians are called in Canada today).

From there it was a short walk to the Fairmont Empress Hotel where they were having high tea. It was 3:30 p.m. when they sat down. Although the cost was over $50.00 per person, they were glad they had splurged. The china was first used in 1939 for the Royal visit of King George VI and Queen Elizabeth.

They started with fresh strawberries, smoked salmon, ham, egg salad, Moroccan Spiced Chicken, and cucumber sandwiches. Then there were scones, shortbread, tarts and several chocolate delicacies. They sat well over an hour sampling and enjoying their food.

After tea they walked across the street to the inner harbor. The temperature was in the mid 70s and they could not have asked for a nicer day. They felt like they were in another world as they walked among the vendors and watched the street performers. Finally, they took a carriage ride to end their day on this magical island. The driver dropped them at the ferry at 6:45 p.m. Tony got the van in line and the others went into the ferry terminal to wait for customs to open and their 7:30 p.m. departure time.

As the boat sailed across the strait, the ninety minutes seemed to zip by. The sunset was once again breathtaking and they soon spied the hotel they had stayed at the night before. They arrived back in Port Angeles at 9:00 p. m. and after clearing U.S. customs were soon driving back towards Seattle.

They had about an hour and a half ride to the Bainbridge Island ferry that would take them to Seattle. Julia and Henry were in the back seat napping while Phoebe and Hugh were quietly talking to each other. Riley kept her eye on the road as Tony drove. The silence between the two of them was very comfortable.

"I am curious, Phoebe, how do you know what to talk about at your meetings."

"Basically I just tell the group the trouble we had getting the right diagnosis and what happened in the early stages. My worst fear was when Dan would get so angry about not remembering and take his keys and slam out the door. Sometimes I would sit for hours waiting for him to come home wondering if he had an accident and had hurt himself or someone else."

"Why didn't you take the keys away from him?"

"I tried that Hugh. One time I hid them but he got in a cab and went to the dealership and had another set made. When I hid that set he physically threatened me. I was so scared I just gave them to him. I could have called the police, but if they took his license away he would have driven anyway. I thought the consequences from him driving without a license would be worse than if he got in a minor accident."

They talked a little longer in subdued voices about her meetings and before they knew it they arrived at the ferry landing.

"I really would like to hear a little more about what you went through. We have to find another time to continue this discussion."

"Phoebe nodded her head in agreement to him. She was a little curious why he was interested but the ferry now beckoned.

They were lucky when they got to the ferry line because the boat was just loading. They thought they might have a good half hour wait but that was not the case. After they had loaded onto the boat they got out of the van and went upstairs. There were lots of seats and watching the lights of Seattle come into view was a beautiful sight. Just before docking they returned to the van, and Tony drove off the ferry. They were right in the heart of the downtown waterfront and they only had a few blocks to drive to the train station.

Phoebe called Charles and he was waiting with the golf cart as Tony parked the van. It was almost midnight and Riley and Hugh waited with Tony until Charles came back from his first run to the Pullman.

They had purposely scheduled Seattle attractions for the next day and a half. They were going to sleep in and leave when everyone was ready. After a whirlwind couple of days they were ready for some leisure time.

Chapter 24

Julia and Henry were awake by 7:00 a.m. because they had napped on the drive back to Seattle the night before. The others did not wake up until 8:00 a.m. By the time they ate breakfast and were on their way it was almost 10:00 a.m. For some reason Phoebe had a hard time getting out of bed, feeling sluggish that morning.

Their first stop was the Seattle Center. Originally built for the 1962 World's Fair, the center has some of Seattle's best attractions including the International Fountain, a Science Center with IMAX, and the famous Chihuly Garden and Glass Museum.

Next they headed to the Space Needle. It is 605 feet tall with a 520 foot high observation deck. They thought they would get a nice overview of the whole city. Hugh mentioned that as you walked around the platform, there were placards listing what you were looking at.

As Tony drove over to the Space Needle, Hugh gave them a short history of the city. "Seattle, with over 650,000 residents, is the largest city in the Pacific Northwest. It was inhabited by Native Americans for at least 4,000 years and named in honor of an Indian chief. Logging was the first major industry, but by the late 19th century the city had became a commercial and shipbuilding center and a gateway to Alaska during the Klondike Gold Rush."

He continued, "The Great Depression damaged the economy, but when Microsoft moved here from New Mexico in 1979 the tech boost began. Amazon, Nintendo, several phone companies and biotech industries spurred the city's growth. I read somewhere that the city has the most expensive real estate in comparison to anywhere in the U.S. For years it was known as the 'Queen City'. There was a contest in 1981 and now the official nickname is the 'Emerald City'. This is in reference to the lush evergreen forests around the area from all the rain."

"I saw that big Ferris wheel last night when we came in on the ferry. What is that all about?" Riley asked.

"The Seattle Great Wheel is one of the largest Ferris wheels in the U.S. It opened in June 2012. It is a new permanent attraction on the waterfront and is open year-round with fully enclosed gondolas. It stands over 175 feet high. After the Space Needle we will head over to the heart of downtown and Pike Place Market. We can buy fresh produce, brought in by the farmers, for lunch. People come there to buy fresh fish. There is even one market where they throw the fish to the customer. You will see street performers entertaining the crowds, and there are many stores and booths where artisans and artist sell their creations."

"That sounds like a lot of fun," Riley added.

"It is," Tony said. "We don't need a big lunch, because then this afternoon we can take a four hour roundtrip cruise to historic Blake Island, the legendary birthplace of Chief Seattle. The cruise itself takes 45 minutes to get to Tillicum Village. When we get there we will learn about Native American culture which was so important to this city, and be able to explore the village. There is also a live performance featuring traditional song and dance and a salmon buffet cooked on outside fires. There are totem poles, and naturally a gift shop we will want to look through. However, I have not booked it, because they said there would be plenty of room and I wanted to make sure everyone wanted to go."

"I think we will pass and go back to the Pullman," Henry said. "We have been there before and Julia and I really enjoy sitting around on the train."

"I have also done it," Hugh said. "But I am looking forward to the boat ride and salmon dinner."

Riley spoke up, "Phoebe and I definitely want to do it. We were reading a brochure when we were on the ferry to Victoria. It sounded like a fun, as well as, educational thing to do."

"Well, it's settled then. The four of us will go. The boat leaves at 4:00 p. m. Julia, you and Henry can take a cab back to the station. Phoebe will give you Charles' number, so he can meet you with the golf cart."

"That sounds great. Julia and I will enjoy having some down time."

"Tomorrow we can go to Pioneer Square," Tony said. "That area is where Seattle's founders first settled in 1852. It has become one of the city's prettiest downtown neighborhoods. The streets are lined with trees with many restored Victorian buildings. It is listed on the Nation Register of Historic Places. The neighborhood gets its name from a small triangular cobblestone plaza officially known as Pioneer Square Park. The park features a bust of Chief Seattle, an ornate pergola, and a totem pole."

Hugh jumped in. "There are some interesting places in that section of town to visit. The Seattle Underground, a network of underground passageways and basements that are remnants of the original city are there. Much of the city was destroyed by a fire in 1889. With the city's hills landfill was brought in and covered up much of the original city. UPS has a beautiful park with a waterfall, and we don't want to miss probably the smallest national park in the U.S. It is dedicated to the gold rush."

Tag teaming as they tended to Tony said, "We thought it would be good after that to go and have a nice lunch in one of those restaurants on the waterfront. It will be an enjoyable way to say good-bye to the city, since the train leaves at 5:00 p.m."

"Phoebe and I were talking and I just want to say we are both so impressed with all the work you two men did for this journey along the coast. The hotels and attractions have been outstanding. I know we keep saying we have to put things on a bucket list and come back but we feel we have really hit the highlights in the limited time we have had. Thank you for all you have done to make this such a wonderful trip."

"To say we could not have done it without you is probably an understatement," Phoebe added.

"And even though we have been here before, all four of you have made this trip so much fun for us. I know Henry will be glad to be on his way tomorrow, as much as he has loved being here. He always worries he will be traveling somewhere and a volcano or earthquake will happen and kill him. He knows it is a very irrational thought, but now he feels he will make it safely home," Julia said with a smile.

Henry blushed when they looked at him. As much as he loved his wife, he wished she had not said anything about his silly fear.

The two men were touched by what the women had said. They had also talked among themselves and agreed that they could not have travelled with anyone more compatible. It had truly been a fun vacation.

They arrived at the Space Needle and Riley, who had been on the lookout, spotted a place to park.

"I hope it is that easy when we get to Pike Place Market," she said.

And it turned out to be. They walked around the market and bought snacks to eat. They were ready to go to the waterfront and started looking for a cab for Julia and Henry. Riley noticed Phoebe had not eaten anything, and asked her if she was alright.

As everyone looked at her, she said, "At first I thought maybe all the hours of touring was getting to me, but I really do not feel very well. I hope I am not getting what you had, Hugh."

"You look very pale, dear." Touching her forehead Julia continued, "You have a temperature."

"I guess we better all go back to the Pullman," Hugh said.

"No. Please I do not want you to do that. I know how much Riley was looking forward to going to Tillicum Village. I don't want you to cancel because of me."

"Look I don't need to go because I have been there before," Hugh said.. "Tony I know you only listed yourself as driver to save money but why don't I take Julia, Henry and Phoebe back to the Pullman. You and Riley can go on the cruise. You haven't been there either and were looking forward to going. With just the two of you it makes more sense for me to take the van, and you two take a cab when you get back. I will be responsible if something happens to the van."

"I trust you, Hugh, but are you sure you don't want us all to come back to the Pullman?"

"No, definitely not. We will be fine. I will take everyone back to the station. While Charles is taking them on the golf cart, I will go to the pharmacy. I spotted a grocery store near the station that will have the medicine Phoebe needs for that temperature. Margaret already expects two for dinner, and one more should not be a problem. We will be fine. Don't worry."

"But what about your salmon dinner, Hugh? You'll miss that," Phoebe said.

"I can have a salmon dinner anytime. It is more important we get you feeling better for the trip home. I will call Charles, so he is waiting for us. He can check with Margaret to see if she needs anything else at the store for dinner"

With everyone in agreement they walked back to the van. Hugh took Phoebe's hand and helped her into the front seat. He could feel that she was burning up and wondered why she had not said anything earlier.

Riley and Tony waved good-bye to the departing van and headed to the waterfront.

Chapter 25

When they reached the pier they each paid separately for their tickets. They still had a half hour before boarding so they browsed the shops on the pier. One in particular was fun. It was called "Ye Olde Curiosity Shop." They learned it was founded in 1899. Besides being a souvenir shop, it looked like an old time museum and had a lot of original Northwest Coast art. The store was very proud of the fact it had been owned by four generations of the same family.

Before long they were in line and boarding the boat. Watching the skyline get farther away Riley mentioned that Hugh seemed very caring towards Phoebe. "Do you think he likes her?"

"He likes her but not in the way you are implying. Hugh's wife was very sick for two years before she died. He took care of her and so he just naturally stepped in when Phoebe became ill. It is in his nature to do that. It is the main reason he will not date anyone seriously again. He does not want to go through being a caregiver ever again. It took a lot out of him."

"That is pretty ironic, because that is exactly how

Phoebe feels. She loved her husband dearly. However after what she went through with him, she has no desire to get serious about anyone either. I do not mean to be nosey but can you tell me what happened to Hugh's wife?"

"I don't think he would mind me telling you. It is not a secret. Hillary had anorexia nervosa. Normally I would not really know much about the disease. But after she died, Hugh started thinking there was something more he should have been able to do to help her. He was really very depressed and after three months of that I dragged him to a bereavement anorexia support group for people dealing with the death of their loved one. Going there I learned a lot, too."

"That was really wonderful of you."

"We have been friends since we were kids and I hated to see him suffer like that. Besides I knew Hillary since college, and she was like a sister to me. Taking Hugh to the meetings turned out to be the best thing that could happen to him at the time. The most important thing we learned was it was not his fault. As with alcoholism, only the person with the disease can choose whether or not to get help."

"I guess that makes sense."

"Yes it does. The one thing family or friends cannot do is blame themselves for their loved one's condition. Since it is psychological, it can only be fixed if the anorexic will accept help. However getting help is not easy, as anorexia is part of the person's identity. Usually the anorexic will not admit there is a problem, especially if they have been denying it for years. So there is no way for them to be cured."

"I had no idea it was that serious. I just thought if they started eating properly again it would go away."

"Unfortunately that is not the case. One man's wife had a heart attack when she started eating normally. Usually the person has a fear of gaining weight along with a distorted body image. Besides getting thinner and thinner the bones lose density. Hillary fell and broke her leg. She had a terrible time healing and was in a wheelchair the last few months of her life. She would also be constantly cold and spent a lot of time in bed under blankets. Even on a hot day she would complain about being cold. That was what killed her. She got into a real hot bath, which the doctors had warned her not to do, and her heart just gave out."

"Now I can understand a little better what it was like for Hugh to go through that."

"Things really got bad about three years before Hillary died. All she thought about was dieting and controlling what she put into her body to the exclusion of her family and friends. She had some weird food rituals including cutting food 'just so' and even with chewing it. By controlling the way she ate, the group taught us that it made her feel stronger and more successful as a person. She obviously had a negative self image, but dieting and losing weight was not going to fix that."

"Couldn't she get some type of help?"

"Hugh tried to get her in counseling, but she refused. She spent her days in excessive exercising and would get intensely anxious, if she could not get her workout in. And she would not go anywhere with Hugh. She spent her day exercising and planning and preparing what she would eat.

She was also good at hiding her habits. No one realized what was happening until the disease had progressed further along. By the time we really noticed something bad was going on, her body was consuming itself from all the self starvation."

"It is hard to believe someone would intentionally do that to themselves."

"I think the thing that helped Hugh get back to normal was when he learned anorexia has the highest mortality rate of any psychiatric disorder. The sad part is only one in ten sufferers get treatment. At that point he quit blaming himself."

"You know I had a wonderful relationship with my husband. I had a hard time dealing with his death. I am afraid to try with someone else because of that. My therapist is helping me deal with those issues. He says risking our hearts is why we are alive. I don't want to look back in regret at the end of my life and be sorry I did not take another chance. I can't imagine how terrible it would be to go through what Phoebe and Hugh have. My pain is nothing compared to what they went through."

"You are probably right about taking a risk, but I think it is a lot easier to just walk your own path with your friends near you. At least that is enough for me. And speaking of paths, the boat is docking and the path awaits us."

Laughing at what he said, the two of them got off the boat and followed the crowd to the festivities. They really enjoyed the village and learned a lot about the cultural heritage and customs of the Northwest Native Americans. They got back on the boat and were in Seattle by 8:00 p.m.

Charles was waiting when the cab dropped them at the train station.

When Riley looked in her room Phoebe was sound asleep from the medicine she had been given. She hoped her friend felt better in the morning. Julia and Henry were in their room, and Hugh was sitting in the parlor reading. They told him about their adventure to the island and they talked about their plans for their last day in Seattle.

It was 9:30 p.m. when Riley went to her room. She was a little tired from the fast pace of the last few days. Saying goodnight to the two men she went to her room and was fast asleep within a half hour.

Chapter 26

It was another sunny day in the Emerald City, and the mountain was out which pleased them on their last day in Seattle.

Everyone was awake and ready to start their day by 8:00 a.m. Everyone, that is, except Phoebe. Her temperature was gone, but she was feeling too weak to go anywhere. She told them to go ahead with their plans for Pioneer Square. They would check with her before noon to see if she wanted to go to the waterfront. Her stomach was not upset and she was actually a little hungry so she thought she might join them for lunch.

Charles took the five of them to the station at 9:00 a.m. Since the Pioneer Square area was right next to the station, they decided to walk. First, they stopped at the Square and then The UPS Park. The park was stunning. It took up a quarter of a block. Trees were planted, so that you could not see inside unless you walked in. Once inside there were tables and chairs, large plants, and a waterfall.

Then they took the underground city tour. On their way back to the station they stopped at the square, looked into a couple of the stores, and stopped at the Klondike

Gold Rush National Park. They building had two levels devoted to the gold rush. Before leaving they watched the thirty minute movie about the Gold Rush with a slant towards Seattle's participation in the event.

It was only a two block stroll back to the station where the van was parked. As they walked, they called Phoebe. She told them she would go to lunch with them. When they got to the station they saw her waiting for them. They all got into the van and headed for the waterfront.

It was a beautiful afternoon.   They went into a restaurant that had seating outside overlooking the water. The mountain was still out. They watched the ferry slowly making its way to Bainbridge Island, as the gulls flew overhead. It was a perfect conclusion to their stay in the Emerald City.

It was 3:00 p.m. when they got back to the station. Tony and Hugh took the van back to the rental agency while the others went to the Pullman. By 4:00 p.m. everyone was on board. The train left at 4:40 p.m. They were all up in the dome car sipping a glass of wine, as the train pulled out of the station.

The train followed Elliott Bay for the next two hours to Everett before starting east and inland. By the time they were eating dinner dusk had arrived and they were headed back into the Cascades.

They had eaten a big lunch which Margaret knew in advance. So the cook had served clam chowder soup and a seafood salad for dinner. It was delicious as usual. Charles made his Brandy Alexander ice cream drink as a sendoff for their West Coast adventure.

Julia and Henry went to their room after they finished their drink. The other four moved to the parlor area and talked about all their escapades so far on the trip. They all wished they could add another couple of weeks to this trip. The time had passed so quickly and there had been so many good times.

Phoebe was not quite back to one hundred percent and found herself getting tired. Looking at her watch she could not believe it was almost 10:00 p.m.. Where had the night gone?

She had liked Riley from their first meeting and now she considered Tony and Hugh friends, too. She had a feeling Riley felt something for Tony and hoped maybe something would happen between the two of them. Tony had been free a long time, and she felt Riley was ready to move on with her life.

She also felt she might like to have a friend to go out with and wondered if Hugh would be agreeable from time to time. She really liked the way he took care of her, including getting medicine, when she was sick. She was not interested in a romance and knew he was not either. Riley had told her about Hugh's wife and she could relate to his feelings. Maybe they could see each other on a no-strings basis when they returned home.

However now it was time to sleep. When she mentioned what time it was and that she was going to bed, they all got up and headed to their rooms. Tomorrow they would arrive in Whitefish, Montana at 7:30 am.

Phoebe would have been surprised to know that Hugh was mulling over the same issues that she had. He was still awake after midnight thinking things over when the train arrived in Spokane. That was where the train coming from Portland hooked onto the Seattle train to continue to Chicago. He felt the vibration when the two trains were coupled together.

As he thought about Tony he realized his friend was feeling more for Riley than he was willing to admit to himself. It would be interesting to see how that situation played out after they arrived home.

And, he decided, he liked Phoebe a lot. She was a very independent woman and was not at all insecure as Hillary had been. If Tony and Riley somehow got together, maybe he and Phoebe could be friends and go out with the other couple. He knew she was not interested in any permanent situation and so he felt safe thinking about being with her. And she was so comfortable to be around. He liked that she had been so responsible, as he had with Hillary, with taking care of her husband under very difficult conditions. And she was such a positive person. As he drifted off to sleep he was thinking maybe they could plan another trip somewhere together.

Chapter 27

6:30 a.m. came early. Everyone was dressed and ready for breakfast at 7:00 a.m. The train was scheduled to arrive at 7:30 a.m. and was running on time for a change. They had their suitcases packed and were ready to get off the train when they arrived at the Whitefish station.

As they exited the Pullman Tony went into the station and they soon saw him returning with a set of keys in his hand. They followed him to a dark blue van. Riley sat in front as usual with her Montana map and they reached Belton at 9:00 a.m.

As they entered the park they were now officially on The Going-To-The-Sun Highway, a fifty mile stretch of road that spanned the park from either the West or East entrances. Phoebe had been given the task of researching the park. As they drove, she began telling them the facts she had learned.

"There are over seven hundred and sixty lakes in the park but only one hundred and thirty one of them are named. This lake on our left is called Lake McDonald. It is the largest lake in the park. It is over ten miles long, one mile wide and 472 feet deep. Our first stop will be at

Lake McDonald Lodge. When we get there we will take a wooden boat ride. I thought that would be a good way to get insider information about the park while enjoying our surroundings.

She then continued, "When we leave the lodge our 'jammer' will fill us in on anything we didn't learn on the boat about the park. We just came in on State Highway 2. The town we passed is called Belton or West Glacier. It is roughly fifty six miles to East Glacier on that highway. We will actually drive that road back to Whitefish when we leave the park. We will return a second time when we ride the train back to Chicago. But we will be traveling in opposite directions, so we should get a different perspective."

"I think I read there are four lodges connected with the park," Riley added.

"Yes, and at one time there were several chalets. Before there were cars the idea was there should be a place to stay no further than a day's horse ride away. Most of the chalets are gone now."

"Will we see the other lodges?" Hugh asked.

"You will. Louis Hill the owner of the railroad had his men help in the construction, and you will be able to see the similarities from what I have read. However, they did not need to construct a lodge at Lake McDonald. In 1895 George Snyder built a small hotel. Ownership eventually passed to John Lewis. In 1910, when Glacier became a park, Lewis built some cabins. Then in 1913 he added to the structure we will see today."

"I am really looking forward to our time here."

"I am, too, Riley; especially after reading up about this park. This lodge is quite unique in the park. Mr. Lewis was a furrier and furnished all the hunting trophies still on display in the lobby. He wanted the mounted animals to give the place a 'hunting lodge' atmosphere. And the huge fireplace adds to the hominess of the lobby. Legend has it that Charles Russell scratched the pictographs that you will see in the base of the fireplace, although this has never been proved. There is a beautiful log dining room and both the dining room and bar look out at the lake."

When they drove up to the lodge, they saw little cabins and several other buildings. But what amazed them was how beautiful the log lodge, with the Swiss chalet atmosphere, actually looked. Upon entering the lobby they saw the large fireplace on the left along with comfortable couches, rocking chairs, and a piano.

There was another door straight in front of them which led down to the lake. Above them was an open area all the way to the ceiling. There were balconies in a square around the upper two levels. They were only about five feet wide; just wide enough for people to walk to their rooms. And there were animal trophies hanging from every level.

They arrived about fifteen minutes before their boat ride so they took a left down the hall past the bar to the dining room and rest rooms.

"I wish we were staying here," Riley said.

"I do, too." Phoebe agreed. "But we only have a couple of days and had to be selective where and what we would see."

After the restroom break they went out the back door. On both sides of the walk, placed against the building, were more rocking chairs and geraniums planted everywhere. It was very inviting. But instead of sitting they kept walking down the path to the lake and the wooden boat they spied.

As they climbed on board the historic wooden boat they learned from the park employee their boat had been built in 1924 and had been operating ever since. Even though the boat held eighty people it was early in the morning and early in the season so it was only half full.

They settled down for their relaxing hour ride on the lake as the guide began to tell them the history of the park.

"The Blackfeet called this area 'The Backbone of the World' and if you get over to the East side of the park, you will see why. The natives aggressively guarded their hunting grounds. Lewis and Clark came near Glacier, but because the weather was overcast it blocked their view. If they had discovered Marias Pass, it would have simplified their journey. From then on the Native Americans guided many visitors over safer but steeper passes. It was not until 1889 that John Stevens finally figured out where the pass was located. This was important because the pass had a lower altitude and easier grade so trains could cross the Continental Divide. Once it was discovered two work camps were set up in East Glacier where Glacier Park Lodge was built and in West Glacier where Lake McDonald Lodge is located."

The six of them listened intently as the guide continued, "Louis Hill and the Great Northern railroad built Glacier Park Lodge between 1911-1913. It was Hill's attempt to develop the West, especially the tourism industry. His slogan was 'See America First.' He had the railroad to get people there but he needed places for the tourists to stay. Since there were not enough workers in the area, bridge and trestle crews were used. Sixty logs were used in the interior. These logs were from 500 to 800 years old when they were cut. Just sitting in the lobby you have to marvel at how this work was accomplished in those early days."

"I hope we will stop there," Tony said as Phoebe nodded "yes."

"The next of the great lodges is Many Glacier. If you guessed it was named for the many glaciers in the area, you are correct. Many Glacier is half way between Glacier Park Lodge and Waterton. The site was chosen for the waterfront as well as the views of the glaciers on the opposite side. Hill had 400 men working day and night from May to September in 1914. The building opened July 4, 1915. If you get to that lodge, you cannot help but marvel at how it could be built in such a remote area. Even the trains did not come close. The workers had to construct a sawmill and their own kiln on the grounds to accomplish their work."

"That is where we will be spending the next two nights," Phoebe whispered to the others.

"The last lodge is in Waterton, in Alberta, Canada. There is only a year round population of fifty people since the town is so remote and so unforgiving in the winter. The Prince of Wales (or the POW as it is known) is a very unique looking building. However inside the rooms are very similar to the other two lodges since Hill's men built it. The building sits 'high on a windy hill' in front of Waterton Lake, and the structure is known to sway in high winds. It is a beautiful lodge and serves afternoon tea, if you get a chance to get there."

"We are definitely going there," Phoebe told the others.

The guide continued, "The hotel has eighty six rooms and is seven stories high. It took Hill thirteen years to get the land leased from the Canadian government but only a year to build. Much of the original furniture was constructed on site from British Columbia cedar. The hotel is at the North end of Waterton Lake surrounded by immense mountains. The beauty takes your breath away. Now you know everything you need to know about the great lodges in the park."

Everyone clapped when the guide finished. He asked who was taking The Going-To-The-Sun Road and everyone raised their hand. He then continued with some geological information about the park.

"I guess I should tell you a little about the road you will travel. First of all remember Glacier National Park was named, not for the glaciers, but for the fact that the glaciers carved out this park. You will be climbing up on the road to Logan Pass. Be sure and make some stops and look behind you at all the U shaped valleys. Those are where the glaciers came through. In another twenty years, with global warming, there may be no more glaciers left only ice fields. But those U shaped valleys will always be there."

Then he continued, "The road you will travel is considered one of the best scenic highways in the world. But it is a two lane road with hairpin turns and very narrow. It took twelve years to build from start to finish. The CCC started construction in 1921. It is only opened all the way through from sometime at the end of June until about mid September. That is because the Logan Pass area gets over eighty feet of snow a year and the threat of avalanches is extreme. Vehicles over twenty one feet long and over eight feet wide are not allowed on the road."

They all looked at each other when he said that. Once again Tony had come through. He realized the van could not go over the road, and he had contacted the Lake McDonald lodge. They had put him in touch with one of the workers who had two days off and wanted to hike in the Many Glacier area.

As soon as they had driven up the boy and his friend were waiting for them. Tony had given him the keys and they were off. They would drive Highway 2 to East Glacier and then take the road to Many Glacier. After parking the van they would give the keys to the front desk.

The two boys planned to hike and stay overnight at employee housing there. The following afternoon they would ride the park shuttle back to Lake McDonald. Tony had given the boys money for their shuttle and $50.00 extra for the driver.

It was 11:00 a.m. when they returned from their boat ride. They walked around a little and then went into the dining room for lunch. Their "Red Bus" ride was starting at 1:00 p.m. and they were all excited after what they had learned from their boat guide.

They were out front just before 1:00 p.m. when two Red Buses pulled up in front of them. The buses had room for thirteen passengers. One person sat in the front with the driver and there were three more seats that held four people each. There were only two other couples assigned to their bus that was going to Many Glacier.

They watched as the two drivers helped each other roll back their tops. There were bars across each seat that kept the tops in place. They would be able to hang on to if they wanted to stand up for pictures when the bus stopped. The driver also placed woolen blankets on each seat in case they got cold.

The driver told them their bus was part of a vintage fleet of thirty three buses from the 1930's. "The Ford Motor Company modernized these buses in 2001 and rebuilt them with flexible fuel engines which operate mainly on propane. Originally the buses were called Red Jammers because of us drivers. The original bus drivers were affectionately known as 'Gear Jammers' or simply 'Jammers' since they had to jam the manual gearbox into low to safely negotiate the steepest road sections. But today, while we are still called 'jammers', the correct terminology for the vehicle is 'Red Bus'."

It was not long after they left the lodge that they stopped at a pull off. They walked down a few steps onto a deck and saw the fast moving Flathead River with two small waterfalls. The rapids were very fast flowing and the river was very noisy. Since the area had been hidden by trees it was an amazing sight to behold.

As they got back into their vehicle the driver told them their elevation was a little over 3,000 feet. They would start climbing now to Logan's Pass. That was the highest elevation in the park for a vehicle at 6640 feet.

As they began ascending they saw avalanche shoots, waterfalls, hairpin turns and, most awesome of all, large U shaped valleys surrounded by mountains. The ride was spectacular and no one talked as they were too engrossed in the views encircling them. There was even a spot called the 'Weeping Wall' where water just came out of the rock like magic.

The jammer stopped about three times along the way so they could stand up and take pictures. Just before arriving at the Logan's Pass parking lot they saw two large mountain goats grazing on the grass. The area was full of cars and motorcycles which seemed surprising. But their driver reminded them that Glacier was mainly a hiking park and there was a very popular trail that began right across the street from where they were parked.

After a brief stop they were on their way again. They had traveled approximately thirty two miles on the Going-To-The-Sun Road and had about eighteen to go. They made one stop where they could see an actual glacier in the distance and another one at St. Mary's Lake. The blue/green color of the water was almost indescribable and they could see a wooden boat in the distance.

They also drove by the mountain the road was named for and their driver said, "One Native American legend tells about the deity Sour Spirit. He supposedly came down from the sun to teach the Blackfeet the basics of hunting. While returning to the sun, an image of Sour Spirit was placed on the mountain as an inspiration for the Natives."

It was not too long after seeing the mountain that they drove by St. Mary's Lodge. They were all sad because they knew their ride was coming to an end. They made a left onto the highway and another left on to the road to Many Glacier. They had climbed out of the mountains and were now in the Great Plains. It was amazing how quickly the scenery had changed.

"The conditions here are very rugged. Not too far from here is an Indian town named Browning. There are times in the winter that the weather is so brutal and the snow so high they have to helicopter food into the people," their guide explained as they started heading back in towards the mountains.

"The road we are traveling on is a little rough," the jammer told them as they just missed a large pothole. "There are several miles on this road to your hotel. It is only open about four months a year because of the weather conditions. East Glacier Lodge is about an hour from here. Basically it was built because that is the closest the railroad could get to here. It is remarkable this hotel could even be erected in this harsh terrain."

"Oh look," Phoebe cried out.

As the Red Bus slowed everyone saw a river on their left, and a black bear sitting in a tree.

"That is astonishing," Riley said in delight.

"You will all love Many Glacier. The hotel, built in the Swiss Chalet style like Lake McDonald, sits on the shores of Swiftcurrent Lake. There is a one hundred and eighty degree view of massive mountains and active glaciers. The scenery is so beautiful there are people who come back year after year. It is a great place to take pictures at sunrise or sunset. Also it is not uncommon to spot mountain goats, bighorn sheep and bears, including grizzlies."

"We saw pictures in our Great Lodges book and are really looking forward to seeing the hotel in person," Phoebe told him.

"You won't be disappointed. And if you do not want to hike, you can ride horseback, rent a boat or even ride a Red Bus to Waterton and the Prince of Wales hotel. There are ranger talks in the evening or you can relax with a drink on the balcony and watch the sunset."

They passed a dam that was built on the river, and soon they were driving up to the hotel. The building was beautiful on the outside and the inside continued the Swiss theme, which blew them away. There was a cozy sitting area in the massive lobby with a large fireplace perfect for sitting and socializing, reading or writing.

There was the same open concept to the ceiling as they saw at Lake McDonald with the square balconies along the walls to the rooms. The difference was the lobby was about four times larger here. And doors and windows faced the opposite side of the entrance overlooking the lake and mountains.

Although it was the largest hotel in the park this was a magical mountain lodge, and it took their breath away. As they walked inside the architecture was stunning. They were so glad they had chosen two nights in this wonderful place.

Since it was just after 3:00 p.m. they were able to check into their rooms. Tony picked up the keys for the van. While everyone else waited Tony and Hugh climbed up a steep hill with a luggage cart to get the suitcases.

Their rooms were nothing special but were clean and they were next to each other. The rooms had the lake view and a connecting balcony with several chairs where they could talk.

Hugh and Phoebe went to explore the hotel while the others unpacked. When they got to the lobby they walked outside to a balcony full of chairs overlooking the lake. Then they retraced their steps and went left at the desk down a long hallway.

On the walls they saw pictures of the hotel and surrounding mountains from the early 1900s. It was amazing to see how much the glaciers had shrunk since that time period. They also saw a cozy little bar and a large dining room with windows all around with views of the lake.

Retracing their steps again they found stairs in the lobby going down to the lower level. There were doors that led right out to the lake. There was also a large meeting room where the ranger talks took place at night. Finally there was a small snack shop where hikers could get all kinds of sandwiches and snacks.

Hugh bought a bottle of wine. They were all tired from their long day, and he thought it would be nice to sit on their balcony and have a drink before dinner.

"Maybe we will see some animals, Phoebe."

"That would just make this perfect day even better."

When they got back to their rooms they all met on the balcony and had their wine.

"You know I could just sit here half the day looking at this scenery," Riley said.

"We have been to many, many places but never here," Julia added. "I think Henry would agree that jammer was totally correct. This is a magical place. I am so happy we were able to come here."

Henry nodded his head in agreement, as they sat in silence for a few minutes just taking in the view.

Suddenly Tony spoke up, "Look over there on the mountains. I believe those are bighorn sheep."

"Now we just need to see a grizzly," Riley said smiling happily.

They had only ordered soup and salads at lunch so they went to an early dinner. They were seated at a table right by the window. To their astonishment two moose were down at the lake drinking. After dinner they went to the ranger talk but by 9:00 p.m. they were in their rooms ready for bed. It had been a jam-packed day but one of the best ones on the whole trip.

Tony stayed up a little while reading but everyone else was asleep not long after they got to their rooms.

Chapter 28

Phoebe woke up at 6:00 a.m. She did not want to waste time sleeping while staying at this extraordinary place. She decided she would take a walk out by the lake.

To her surprise she ran into Hugh in the lobby with the same thought in mind. "Great minds," he smiled at her. They went down to the lower level and out the doors to the lake. They saw two canoes paddling to the other side as they headed left out of the hotel. The sun was angled just right, and they saw the reflection of the giant mountains surrounding them in the water.

"I wish I had brought my camera. That would make a beautiful picture."

Phoebe nodded in agreement.

Continuing their walk they spied more moose across from them drinking and eating from the branches growing along the shore.

"I wonder if those are the same ones we saw at dinner last night?"

"Probably," Hugh decided.

They continued walking for about a half hour without speaking. The quietness was captivating. They ran into some other walkers, but no one was talking. Everyone seemed immersed in the beauty of their surroundings.

I am probably enjoying just being around Hugh more than I should Phoebe started thinking to herself. He is such an easy going man. He was so thoughtful when I was sick. I know he took care of his wife but it was really nice of him to get me medicine and see to Julia and Henry. I don't think Riley and I could have found more congenial men to come on this trip than we did.

After all the drama with Dan it's nice to have someone calm to be around. I know I don't want to get involved again, but my stomach gets a little jumpy when I see him. I look forward to our time together. He really seems interested in what I went through with my husband. I wonder if he will open up about his wife. Although our situations were different, from what Riley says, we both faced similar ordeals. I guess time will tell.

With a sigh Phoebe looked at Hugh and he automatically turned to head back.

Wow, it is almost as though he can read my mind. That is amazing. But I have to quit thinking these thoughts. We are hopefully friends, and that is all we will ever be.

As they walked back to the lodge, they saw Riley and Tony on the balcony watching for them. They waved as they went in through the lower level doors. Climbing the stairs they also saw Julia and Henry in the lobby. It was 7:30 a.m. and they all walked together down the hall for breakfast in the dining room.

"Where did you go, Phoebe?"

"I woke up early and decided to go for a walk. It was so peaceful out by the lake. I ran into Hugh on my way so we went together," she told her friend.

There was a breakfast buffet in the dining room and they thought that would be the quickest way to eat. After breakfast they went back to their rooms to collect their belongings. Tony went for the van, since he had brought what he needed to breakfast.

By 8:15 a.m. they were on their way to Waterton. It took a little over an hour with the stop at customs to get to Waterton Lakes National Park.

As they came into town they saw Columbia ground squirrels popping their heads up from their underground tunnels, where they lived. The town itself sat right next to the lake and the main street ran three blocks with a motel, restaurants and some shops.

There were some cute little cottages where the residents lived, but most amazing were the mule deer running all over town munching on people's grass. After passing by several deer they arrived at the boat landing.

They could see the POW sitting up a high hill on their left. It was a very unique building, hard to describe. They went into the ticket office and purchased the two and a fourth hour round trip tour to Goat Haunt in the United States. Once again they were riding a wooden boat; this one built in 1923.

The area had some of the most spectacular mountain scenery in the Rocky Mountains. As the boat cruised the shoreline of upper Waterton Lake they could see majestic towering cliffs, unique geological formations, beautiful waterfalls, and snow clad mountain peaks. It was an incredible view of the region and they were amazed by the beauty.

They learned that the Montana and Alberta Rotary Clubs had gotten together to push for the creation of this first ever international peace park anywhere in the world. Because they were out in the middle of the wilderness, there was no way to tell if you were in the U.S. or Canada. Since this was the case it seemed appropriate for the two nations to agree to work together to preserve the whole area.

They crossed the 49th parallel and went back into the U.S. But they would not have known this unless the guide had told them. The boat stopped briefly and they looked at the mountains on both sides. It was obviously bigger than it looked but it seemed as if someone had run a large lawn mower up both sides of the mountain. That was the only way they knew they had crossed the border back into the U.S.

The boat arrived at Goat Haunt; a drop off for the hikers. They spent about fifteen minutes walking the shoreline, and then headed back to Waterton. On the way back a moose swam across in front of the boat, and they saw two black bears on the shoreline.

After the boat returned to Waterton they stopped at the hotel before going back to Many Glacier. They had decided not to eat lunch at the POW, because they had a big breakfast and were planning dinner in the dining room again.

However the English feel of the hotel was very appealing. Tony mentioned he loved bangers and mashed and Henry said he would have had fish and chips, if they had eaten there. The bellmen all wore kilts and were very accommodating. The travelers sat in the lobby in front of the large picture window enjoying the magnificent panoramas of Waterton Lake along with the surrounding mountains they had just seen on their boat ride.

They stopped briefly in the gift shop and bought the book, *High on a Windy Hill,* which told the history of the hotel. They thought it would make good reading on the train ride home. By 1:30 p.m. they were on their way back to Many Glacier.

As they were driving back on the road into their hotel, they were treated to another incredible site. They passed a large meadow on their right and out from the tress came a mother grizzly bear with two cubs following her. They knew she was a grizzly by the large hump on her back. They were glad they were not walking outside, or they might not have lived to tell the tale. They pulled over and watched fascinated until the bears disappeared back into the trees.

When they got back to the hotel Julia and Henry went to rest. The other four had booked a one and a half hour horseback ride. The ad had read "There is no better way to view the 'Jewel of the Continent' than to see the sites while horseback riding." When they returned they agreed it had been a wonderful experience.

Before going to her room Riley went down to the snack shop to buy a bottle of wine. They had decided they did not want a drink at the indoor bar when they could sit on their balcony and enjoy the scenery.

They had dinner reservations for 7:00 p.m. After taking showers and cleaning up they met for an hour on the balcony and sipped wine while discussing their new adventure. It was the perfect end to another awesome day.

Tomorrow they would head back to Whitefish and then continue their trip on the Pullman for the last leg of their journey back to Chicago.

Chapter 29

The next morning Riley and Tony joined Hugh and Phoebe on their lake walk. They met at 7:00 a.m. and did not get back until after 8:00 a.m. They joined Julia and Henry in the restaurant and had a leisurely breakfast. It was 10:00 a.m. before they left the hotel. None of them wanted to leave and they all hoped that they could come back here someday.

They watched closely as they drove the road back out to the highway but there were no animal sightings that morning. Because they were in a van, they could not take the short cut road over to Glacier Park Lodge. Instead they drove way out on the Plains to the town of Browning before cutting back on Highway 2 to East Glacier.

"Wow! Look at that," Riley said from the front seat as they left Browning heading back West. They all looked to where her finger was pointing. In front of them the Rocky Mountains were coming back into view. They all realized why the Blackfeet called the area "the Backbone of the World." Stretched as far as they could see both to the right and left the mountain looked like a large spine.

"I am sure glad we got to come here and see that. We

might have noticed it on the train but only if we looked backwards," Riley remarked.

They continued watching the mountains get closer, and soon they were in East Glacier. They stopped at the lodge to see what it looked like. Now they could say they had visited all the park lodges. They discovered Glacier Park Lodge was just as spectacular in its own right as the others and they were happy they had stopped. The huge logs in the lobby created a spectacular scene that was completely different from the other hotels.

They made a quick bathroom stop and then got back in the van. They had almost sixty miles of winding road to get to West Glacier and then another forty five minute ride from there. The drive along Highway 2 is one of the most beautiful roads in America and they were looking forward to the sights.

The mountains were all around them and sometimes the river was on one side and sometimes on the other side. They saw the train tracks which also ran on one side of the road and then the other. There were some snow sheds up in the mountains over the tracks which had obviously been built so that the trains could protect themselves in a snow storm or avalanche.

As they continued along Julia sat in the back seat thinking about this part of their journey. She had always loved going to new places and wondered how she and her husband had missed coming to this park. As she looked at Henry she realized he was napping. She smiled at him with the deep love she felt for this man.

Unbelievably they had known each other over eighty

years. They had lived across the street from each other growing up, and their mothers had been best friends. Even though Henry was a year ahead in school, they had always played together. They did not always get along. But they say opposites attract and she realized that was true. At times they clashed, but as they got older they realized neither one of them was all right or all wrong; they just had different opinions.

Life with Henry had never been boring that was for sure. They had their ups and downs. Losing their only child had been the most tragic day in their life, but it had brought them even closer together. Although the intense pain had been with them for a long time her niece, Phoebe, had helped bring light back into their lives.

As she sat musing she watched the awesome scenery at the same time. She was sorry Henry was napping, but she could tell he tired more easily lately. Age was definitely catching up with both of them. However, she knew he would get another chance to view this beautiful scenery when he was on the train ride home. And she would make sure he did watch it then. Truthfully there were probably not many more adventures the two of them would enjoy.

As she continued reflecting about this trip, she thought how interesting it was the way the two men and women had tended to team up. All four insisted they were not looking for a romance, but they had seemed to pair up despite their protests. She knew Riley had dated Hugh, and yet she and Tony seemed to click. It was obvious they enjoyed each other's company.

Although they were not aware of it, apparently Phoebe and Hugh were becoming friends. She wanted to tell them all that they might only get one or two chances at happiness and they needed to grab it when it came. But she knew it was a little too soon to say anything. Journeys can bring people together who otherwise might never have met, as these four were experiencing. As they talked to the others they revealed facts about themselves and slowly grew to know and respect each other.

Julia knew it was important to balance power and control. If one person is always in control in the relationship, the other person begins to disappear. She and Henry had always had a great relationship. They respected each other's opinions and never tried to force their viewpoints on the other. They talked things out and often compromised when it was needed.

But she also realized from talking to her niece that both men had problems with their marriages, and it had scarred them. Hopefully if they took it slow, they would come to realize these women were perfect for them.

She knew this was true from her observations when they were all together. There was a lot of teamwork and give and take and that was the making of good relationships. She just hoped they would come to realize the chance they were being given for happiness. But, of course, only time would tell.

Julia especially wanted her niece to find happiness again. Phoebe's last few years had been so difficult. She hoped Phoebe would find someone to love and treasure her again; someone she could have fun with and laugh with.

They were about forty five minutes past their last stop when the van made a left hand turn. It was almost 1:00

p.m. From the front seat she heard Riley say, "Wake up everyone. Tony and I thought we should stop for a quick lunch, or we will be starved by dinner."

"Is this the Isaac Walton Inn?" Phoebe asked. "I know you mentioned a possible stop here."

"Yes it is. This is an historic inn and was built to house the railroad workers since it is about half way between East and West Glacier."

As they drove down the road the Inn came into view.

"Wow, it looks like a train car," Hugh said.

"It is supposed to," Riley agreed. "Tony thought it would be a nice stop. We will actually pass by here on the train home. It is not a set stop, but if anyone rides the train and wants to get on or off, the train makes a stop here. From what I read it does that a lot in the winter during the ski season."

Continuing on she told everyone what she had read about the place. "Besides this main inn they also have old caboose cars you can stay in with authentic railroad paraphernalia. This hotel is open year round, unlike the park lodges. They even have ski in and out cabins right on the trail system. There is also a dining car they use as a restaurant. That is where we are headed now."

Julia was thinking what a great stop this was. Now Henry would be awake for the rest of the drive. She knew he would so enjoy the upcoming scenery.

They climbed the stairs to get into the Inn and had lunch in the dining car. They were not really hungry and did not want to spoil their dinner, so they ordered soup. Each couple split a piece of pie. It was just enough to take the edge off the men's hunger pangs.

After lunch they explored the Inn. They walked upstairs and noticed, although the hallway was wider, it appeared you were walking down the hallway in an actual train car. Then they went down to the lower level where the bathrooms were located. They saw a bar and a place to play board games along with lots of railroad items from the old days.

As they got back into the van, they were all happy they had made the stop. The rest of the journey continued without interruption. Julia and Henry were holding hands as the beautiful scenery unfolded in front of them. They smiled at each other when they saw a mountain goat out their window. When they drove by West Glacier they did not stop. Instead they continued on to Whitefish.

Tony dropped everyone off at the station and then went to return the van. The town was not very big with less than 7,000 population. However, it grew for two reasons. Building the railroad through the city helped the development of the city. Railroad workers settled there and a logging industry also spurred the economy.

Then in the 1940s a ski resort was built on the Big Mountain. By the mid 2000s almost 70,000 people got on or off at the station every year for skiing in the winter or going to the park in the summer. Obviously, this made for a very economically stable town.

Since this region was part of the Wild West, after unpacking while Julia and Henry rested, the other four decided to window shop along the four block town and have a drink in a local saloon.

It was a fun way to spend the rest of the afternoon. Tomorrow they would be back on the Pullman for the three day and two night journey back to Chicago. As much as they enjoyed the Pullman, it was also nice to spend some time walking in an authentic Western town.

Margaret and Charles outdid themselves for dinner that night. There was a park right across the street from the train station with grills. While they were staying in Glacier their two attendants had gone to the store and bought everything they needed for a steak dinner with all the trimmings. Charles planed to grill their dinner. He also bought ice cream. This would be the last time he would make his Brandy Alexander's for everyone.

Charles had told the four of them there would be a surprise for dinner. He called Phoebe's cell when it was time for them to head back to the Pullman.

When they returned from downtown Julia and Henry were enjoying a glass of wine in the living room area. All six of them went up to the dome car where salads were waiting. As the dinner progressed they looked out at the Big Mountain and watched as the sun set. It was the last of all the beautiful moments on their trip. Tomorrow they would be heading home.

Meanwhile the steak, baked potatoes, and asparagus were enjoyed by all. After dinner as they drank their brandy drinks, they were all sad the journey was coming to an end. They had no idea something else lay in store for all of them.

Chapter 30

It was 8:00 a.m. when the train pulled out of the Whitefish station. They were fifteen minutes late due to the need to couple the Pullman but the conductor knew they could easily make up that time.

They were all in the dome car having breakfast, as the train departed. Although they made up a little time, they were still fifteen minutes late when the train left West Glacier. Close to one hundred passengers had gotten off at West Glacier to spend time in the park.

This was pretty normal for that time of the year. Charles had also been told there were two tour groups of almost one hundred travelers getting on at East Glacier for the trip home. This would delay them a little more, but the conductor was confident they would not be late getting back to Chicago unless something unexpected happened.

As they continued, they saw the road they had travelled the previous day. However now they were going the opposite direction and the scenery seemed a little different. They were enjoying the gentle rocking and swaying of the car as it chugged along the tracks.

There were fifty six miles between East and West Glacier along this set of tracks. They had come almost fifteen miles from their stop in West Glacier. To their north a river was flowing with the mountains beyond that. On their right was a small cliff that covered the windows of the train, so there was no view.

Henry got out of his seat and started down the stairs to go to the bathroom when a small bump occurred. It did not really register in their minds, but for some reason it put their senses on alert. As he continued down the next step a violent shaking started. He turned to look back at Julia while trying to hang on and saw her eyes widen. Somehow he knew this would not end well.

As the shaking continued for what seemed like an eternity, but in reality was only about eighteen seconds, Henry tumbled down the rest of the steps hitting the back of his head. Julia tried to get up, but the train was shaking so hard she could not get out of the booth.

Finally the shaking stopped. Everything was unnaturally quiet, since the train had come to a full stop. Julia and Phoebe both went down to Henry. He was unconscious, but at least he wasn't dead.

Just then the shaking started again. Riley and the men watched in horror, as a rock slide took out part of the mountain and covered the front of the train and the road. Meanwhile, part of the cliff to their right fell on the train. The only cars not covered were their Pullman and the crew car in front of them.

Once again silence descended except for the distant cries they knew were the people trapped in the rest of the train. Both the conductor and his assistant were in the crew car when the earthquake hit. Since they had been sitting at a table, they were not hurt. The conductor sent his assistant through the train to assess the damage and gather the passengers. Meanwhile, he got on his walkie talkie to the West Glacier station to ask for assistance.

Charles had been given a walkie talkie for emergencies and he learned what was taking place from the conductor. He had let the man know they had an unconscious passenger, but that the others were safe. Then he told everyone what was happening.

They put blankets around Henry, as Julia held him in her lap. However there was nothing else they could do for him until helped arrived. Phoebe sat with her aunt while the others stayed in the dome car. Margaret and Charles joined them since the conductor had said that was probably the safest place in case of more aftershocks. Meanwhile, they watched as the unhurt travelers started exiting out of the crew car and sat down next to the track.

They did not know it, but there were five other travelers and three crew members who had been hurt on the train. However, no one was hurt as badly as Henry. The others had been walking around when the earthquake struck and had broken bones from their falls. The rest of the crew assisted in helping those people to the crew quarters.

The conductor did not want any of the injured to sit outside. Since the crew car was not covered with cliff debris he thought it would be the safest car for them. After everyone was removed from the rest of the train, he had the car uncoupled from the other part of the train. He was hoping an engine could be sent to at least take the Pullman and the crew car back to West Glacier.

They weren't sure how long they would have to wait for help, but luck was riding with them. In a little less than an hour three school buses came into view. There was a rafting company that was not using their buses at that time, so they sent them to get the passengers back to West Glacier. It was obvious no one would be continuing forward.

Going east was not really an option. There was a small hotel about seven miles up the road and then another six miles to the Isaac Walton Inn. East Glacier was another thirty miles past that. No one knew what the road conditions were like in that direction. Going back west was the only logical choice.

The injured were the first to be loaded onto a school bus with their companions. Julia gave Phoebe a hug, as the loaded bus began the journey back to West Glacier. Ambulances from the hospital at Whitefish had been notified so they would be waiting when the bus reached the train station.

The Amtrak travelers had priority boarding. After dividing the crew between the three buses and loading the passengers on the remaining two, there was absolutely no room for the Pullman travelers. As it was the crew had to stand in the aisles, and the conductor thought that was too unsafe for any travelers.

The conductor was like a ship's captain. He had to stay until the last passenger was safely removed. Two other crew members volunteered to stay with him and the six people from the Pullman.

It was a little unnerving watching the last bus pull out, but they knew it would only be an hour before one of them returned.

Chapter 31

Margaret went to the kitchen and got glasses of ice tea and cookies for everyone. The conductor had come by to let them know he was going to the front of the train to assess the damage.

They sat in the dome car and watched as he walked towards the front of the train. Meanwhile, the other two crew members went exploring to the west along the side of the river. They could see them off in the distance when the next aftershock hit. For some reason this one seemed worse than the other two.

They watched as the front section of the uncoupled train fell over, as the road gave way. They had a bad feeling the conductor had been crushed by the train. Meanwhile, they saw a large crack open up in the earth behind them. The crewmen started running west as fast as they could. They were stumbling and trying to avoid the mountain that was coming down on top of the road behind them. Since the road was blocked to the west, they had no idea if the crewmen made it through.

With the wide chasm that had appeared behind them and a mountain of dirt beyond that they realized their exit to the west had been cut off. They were in shock over the terror of what they had just witnessed.

Charles told them to stay put in case of another aftershock. He tried the walkie talkie but got no response so he climbed out of the Pullman. They watched him as he started forward. They waited over fifteen minutes.. Tony and Hugh were just starting to go after him, when they saw him walking back. There was no one with him but at least he was safe.

The men met him as he climbed back into the car. He told them there was no sign of the conductor. He could only see the top of the train because it was lying on its side and the dirt from the cliff and the road had mostly covered it. It was obvious the conductor had been crushed under the train when it fell sideways during the latest quake.

He suggested they meet in the dome car and discuss the situation. He knew it was important the women also know what they were facing. But first he wanted to check on something.

They watched Charles as he climbed the dome car stairs with a set of keys in his hand.

"I don't know how long it will take until we are rescued. However I want to assure all of you we are relatively safe here, as long as any aftershocks don't damage the Pullman. I would like to believe they will send a rescue team soon. They have helicopters in Whitefish for mountain rescues so I would think they would send one for us."

Then he added, "I just want everyone to know that we have plenty of food supplies since we had taken on extra for the trip home. If help does not come by tomorrow, we will go into the Empire Builder and raid their kitchen of canned goods and any nonperishable items we can use. The most important thing is we have a backup generator. I think we should only keep it on for cooking and at night for light and heat so it does not run out of fuel."

They all were nodding in agreement with what he was saying. "Water will also not be a problem. We have a river down there to tap if need be. As long as we boil the water it will be fine for drinking. Lastly I want everyone to know about these keys in case something would happen to me. The most important key on this ring is for the gun cabinet."

They all looked at him with questioning stares. "Todd had two rifles and one pistol locked in a gun cabinet, in case we ever needed to hunt for food in an extreme emergency. He even placed a couple of fishing poles in there. I am not concerned about food. I don't know how much of this area has been disturbed by the quakes but my real concern is the bears, especially the grizzlies. And trust me they will smell our food. We need to keep one rifle in the downstairs parlor and one in the kitchen. That is where the two doors to get in here are located."

"Now you have us scared," Hugh said.

"I don't mean to frighten you, but we all need to be on high alert. We need to take this threat very seriously. If we have to start shooting at them, they might give up. In the daylight we need one person in this dome car watching all the time. We will all take turns an hour at a time. But that person needs to be paying attention and not reading or chatting; just watching. At night when it is dark we need one person sitting by each door in three hour shifts. I am not concerned if you doze a little because you will definitely hear them, if they try to break in."

"But I have never shot a gun," Phoebe said as Riley also shook her head "no."

"How about you two men?"

"Actually we went on an African safari years ago and had to learn for that trip," Hugh answered.

"Well we have lots of ammunition so I want you two men to take some practice shots just to get used to the feel of the rifles. Then each of you take a woman, and start teaching them how to shoot. If a bear does come during their watch, they can yell for us. I know none of us will sleep very deeply with the ongoing threat. But in an emergency I want them to be comfortable pulling the trigger. And I don't want the two women to have door watch at the same time."

Phoebe and Riley were not thrilled with the idea of using a gun, but the threat of a possible grizzly attack outweighed their fear of shooting.   Margaret dug some used cans out of her recycle garbage and the four went outside by the river to start practicing.

Unbeknownst to them the two crew members had made it safely past the crumbling mountain and had run into the school bus returning to get everyone. The last view they had witnessed was the front of the train tipping over with the mountain falling on top of it. They told the bus driver they were sure no one could have survived that event.

Since the earthquake had affected the whole area, the bus was desperately needed back in town for ongoing medical needs. The driver did drive up to the large chasm in the road. Beyond that half of the mountain had fallen over the highway.

There was not a thing he could do about the situation at the present. He would report when he got back into town. They could send a helicopter to fly over the site, but frankly he agreed with the crew men it was probably hopeless that anyone was left alive in that region.

By the time he returned to West Glacier he was immediately sent to the Whitefish hospital with more injured people. A lot of help was needed with the disaster and every able bodied man or woman was pressed into service. The two crew men assuming the ambulance driver had reported in went about helping where they could.

With no one knowing what had really happened the six people on the Pullman were totally forgotten. There were far more critical situations to deal with as several smaller aftershocks rocked the region throughout the night.

Chapter 32

After the men were fairly confident the women could shoot the rifles if necessary, they went back to the Pullman placing the guns where Charles had suggested. Margaret made some soup and sandwiches for lunch, but no one was really hungry.

Charles did not think a threat of a bear attack would occur in daylight, but they still started their rounds of watching. Phoebe and Hugh went to their bedrooms to rest while Tony sat with Riley. She had the first hour and he the second, so they decided to spend the two hours together.

For lack of anything better to do he started telling her in more detail about his marriage to Ginger. Riley had no idea how difficult it was to live with a compulsive spender. The strange thing was he thought they had a good marriage at first. It wasn't until later that he discovered all she had done to hide her addictive behavior from him.

"You know, Tony, maybe you shouldn't be afraid to find someone else to love. It has been a long time since you went through all your trials with Ginger. Even you have admitted you thought you had a good marriage up to a point."

"You are probably right, Riley. But I keep worrying about finding someone I love, and then they go off the deep end like Ginger."

"In a way I can understand that but in a way I can't. You are much older now. If you find someone closer to your age, chances are they will be matured enough that addictions would not be a problem. I cannot believe if the new person did suffer from some sort of addiction, you would not be sensitive enough after what you went through to recognize the signs."

"I had never really considered that. I have seen a lot of my men friends getting divorced over the years, but you are right. Mostly they are the men who marry much younger women and they seem to grow apart."

"All I know is Jake and I had a great marriage. We certainly had our ups and downs, but we always talked through our problems and compromised when needed. It wasn't perfect. It was just good. I guess in a way I am like you. I am afraid to try and meet someone new. What if they were controlling or did not want to compromise, and I did not discover that until after we married. I don't want to go through a bad marriage."

The two of them were sitting across from each other, but they were not really looking at each other. They had their eyes on the horizon. Maybe it was easier for them to talk about their feelings while they were looking elsewhere.

"My psychologist has an interesting quote. He says, 'When the door of happiness closes another opens; but often times we look so long at the closed door, we don't see the new one that has opened for us.' I never really believed him, but lately it does have me thinking. Maybe he is right."

"Well that is an interesting quote. I would think it also helps to have a positive attitude. I have a friend who always says 'A happy person can enjoy the scenery while on a detour.' Hopefully we are happy people because we definitely have the scenery to enjoy and apparently we are on a detour. Listen we still have another forty five minutes on our watch. How about I turn on some oldies on the satellite radio? Since it looks as though we could be stuck here awhile we can talk more about relationships another time."

"Music would be nice, but what about the backup generator giving out?"

"Hugh has some expertise with generators and fuel. Tomorrow he and Charles are going through the train to see if they can check the engine. They are hoping they can use the train diesel if they need it."

"That would be a relief to know. If we are stuck here on this detour, we could at least survive with food, water and electricity. But hopefully it will not be forever," she said with a twinkle in her eye.

The time went quickly and then it was Phoebe's turn to watch. They had decided Margaret should not have to be part of the daytime watches, since she had to fix the meals. Tony and Riley went to their rooms to relax. Everyone wanted to rest when they could, since they would also be covering the overnight hours.

Phoebe's time went quickly. About fifteen minutes before her time was up, Hugh arrived.

"Do you really think the bears will show up, Hugh?"

"I don't know. But have you ever seen a picture of a grizzly? When they are standing up on their hind legs they can be ten feet tall. Probably that may be an exaggeration, but I know they can weigh several hundred pounds. You would not stand a chance, if one came at you."

"I will take your word for that. I guess I have no interest in seeing bears in pictures or for real."

"I have some other good news. Charles has been searching through all the drawers, nooks, and crannies. In a kitchen cupboard, way up high, he discovered three cans of bear spray. That might also come in handy. He does not want anyone to go outside without carrying a can in their pocket. If you get too close to shoot the gun, the spray will definitely be useful. Do you want to stay and keep me company for a little bit? You promised you would tell me more about your husband's ordeal and it is a little boring sitting here."

"Actually I was going to my room to rest as Charles said we should but I am really not tired. So I would be happy to keep you company for awhile."

"You told me about the driving incident with your husband, but what other things do you talk about at your meetings?"

"Basically I just tell them a little of what happened in my life. I do an overview of what I went through and talk about fifteen minutes. I have found that since every case is different it is more productive to talk awhile and then take questions. That way I can talk specifically to the issues facing the particular people in that group. But I don't talk alone. There is usually a man I am teamed up with, so people can get the perspective of a man who had to deal with his wife. There is also a psychologist and someone from the particular county who knows what services are available."

"That sounds like it is really a useful meeting."

"Yes it is. A lot of times people come up to you afterwards and just want to talk. It does not really help them except sometimes they just need someone to listen to what they are going through. I certainly don't have a lot of answers. I only know what worked or did not work for me in certain situations. But having a shoulder to cry on can be very positive."

"You are right about that. I know Tony told Riley about my wife and she probably told you."

Nodding her head "yes" he continued. Hillary kept everything hidden so well I never really knew anything was wrong until it was too late. After that she just spiraled down and there was nothing I could do. It would have been nice to have a group counseling session, like you participate in, when I was going through things with Hillary. But quite honestly I would never have gone to one at the time. I kept blaming myself thinking there was more I could do for her. I did not realize she was the only one who could change her actions. Then suddenly she was dead, and our life together was over."

"That had to be terrible for you."

"It was, mainly because I thought I was at fault somehow.

And to be honest I would have probably continued to feel that way. I would never have considered counseling, if Tony had not dragged me to a session. When I started hearing the stories I could not believe how alike they were to mine. It took awhile, but I finally realize nothing was my fault. Hillary was the one with the low self esteem and she did it to herself. I learned that people suffering from anorexia, as well as other addictions, are experts at hiding what they are doing."

"You know it is strange, but we both had to deal with abuse. My husband lashed out at me physically several times. One time when he was in the shower I thought he might really hurt me. I know he did not realize what he was doing, but it really scared me. While your abuse from Hillary was not physical, you still went through a lot of emotional abuse. That is why you kept blaming yourself. I'll bet she turned things around several times to make it look as though you were at fault."

"It is amazing that you know that. She did exactly what you said."

"One thing I have learned is, as bad as physical abuse is, emotional abuse can be just as damaging to the spirit. I am so glad you went for counseling. Neither one of us wants to have another commitment, because of the terror we went through with our spouses. I understand exactly where you are coming from."

Hugh looked at her curiously. She was right. He had no desire to connect with someone, but she was the first person who really understood what he had gone through and how h felt. If he ever did want a relationship, it would have to be someone like her who would understand what he went through.

"This conversation has gotten much more serious, than I intended. I thought we would just chat a little, but we really talked about some deep issues."

"Not quite a light conversation about bears like you planned," she said laughing at him.

"Hardly."

"But changing the subject, I wonder why a helicopter hasn't flown overhead to check out this train."

"Who knows? They might be very busy with medical emergencies, and just assumed we all got out."

"That could be, but I am still surprised Aunt Phoebe did not alert anyone."

"That does seem odd, doesn't it?"

What they did not know, and would not learn until much later, was Henry had been hurt a lot worse than they suspected. He had hit his head harder than they imagined. After he had gotten to the hospital, he had slipped into an irreversible coma. Julia had been inconsolable.

They had hooked him up to a breathing machine which was the only thing keeping him alive. His prognosis offered no hope for recovery. That evening Julia slipped into his bed and held him in her arms one last time. She knew there was no way she would stay in this world without him.

As the sun was rising she kissed his cheek, turned off his machine, and as he took his last breath, so did she. When the nurse came in to check on him that morning she found both of them lying peacefully together in bed. There was no sign of life from either of them. They were now together for eternity.

Julia had given the hospital Phoebe's cell in case of emergency, but naturally she did not answer. No one had any idea she and the others were stuck in the middle of nowhere with no cell service available.

Chapter 33

They were very subdued at dinner. Charles and Riley had been assigned the first door watches from 9:00 p.m. until midnight. Phoebe and Tony had the next three hours. From 3:00 a.m. to 6:00 a.m. it would be Hugh and Charles again.

Charles did not mind taking a double shift. At 6:00 a.m. Margaret would handle the door by the kitchen while she prepared breakfast. Charles would eat a little something and then go back to sleep for a few hours. Riley, Phoebe and Tony would take turns sitting by the parlor door each morning until daylight. As soon as it was light enough, they would move to the dome car until 8:00 a.m. when the daylight duty of one hour shifts would commence again.

Actually sitting by the doors was not too hard of an assignment. You could read if you wanted. It was just a matter of listening. However you had to keep your eyes on the outdoors during the daylight watches in the dome car. Not counting meals that left the five of them with two one hour shifts a day.

In the daylight the bears might come to the river to drink or fish and it would be easy to see them from that distance. Then it was just a matter of time for them to come to explore the train, especially if they smelled food cooking.

The morning went well. Hugh and Charles went to check the train for food supplies and see about the diesel. They left Tony with the women in case a problem developed. They were able to bring back quite a bit of food and knew they would not go hungry for quite a long time.

Since the weather warmed up quite a bit after lunch, they decided they needed to bathe. They did not want to waste their drinking water for this. So the three women went to the river with soap and towels as Charles stood watch. He crossed the river at a narrow place and looked at the mountains, so as not to be watching the women as they cleaned themselves.

Next the two men got in the river and after they were clean they stood watch while Charles took his turn. Bears could run very fast and come out of nowhere, so Charles felt it was important to have the gun and bear spray constantly ready.

By the third morning after the quake everyone was beginning to wonder why they couldn't let their guard down. But Charles was insistent. He told them if they made it through one more night without an attack they could discuss watch changes tomorrow morning.

It did not help that they were all on edge wondering if assistance would ever arrive. That night everything remained quiet. At 3:00 a.m. Hugh and Charles took over their shifts. They had been trading door duty and Charles was in the parlor. At 4:30 a.m. he heard a rattling on the stairs and called to Hugh.

They both held their rifles ready watching the door. Phoebe heard them and came running. She picked up the bear spray. A huge grizzly appeared at the back door. He stood up on his hind legs and looked in at them. He was taller than the door in that position and they heard his claws rattling the door handle.

Phoebe did not think she could be any more scared than she was. Her teeth were chattering and she clutched the can of bear spray so tightly her knuckles turned white. Just then the door opened and she heard the roar of gunfire. Both guns went off at the same time, and the bear fell backwards off the train.

They waited five minutes to make sure he did not move. Then the three of them pushed the body until it rolled down the slight hill towards the river. By the time they got back into the Pullman everyone else was awake.

At that point Phoebe was shaking and was obviously in shock. Hugh put his arms around her and sat with her on the couch. He talked quietly to her until her shaking abated. Tony and Riley watched anxiously until she calmed down.

"Riley do you mind taking Phoebe back to her bedroom and staying with her a little. Tony has some Advil PM and we will give her one. That should help her sleep for awhile." Hugh said.

Nodding at him, Riley took Phoebe to her room, as Tony went to get the pill. Coming back in the parlor he heard Charles saying they probably did not need to worry about another attack until at least daylight.

At that point Margaret went back to her room, too. Hugh convinced Tony to try to get some sleep. He had just done the middle shift and it was important he be fresh in the morning in case of attack.

By 7:30 a.m. everyone was up. Phoebe felt a little groggy from the pill, but she was afraid to sleep any longer. Charles should have been tired, but his adrenalin was on high alert. As soon as it was light enough, they went up to the dome car.

The dead bear was gone! At least they had thought he was dead. Since Charles had been riding on these Western rails for years he had studied bear behavior in case he ever encountered one. He knew the bear was dead. He also knew that there would be one or two other bears who would be upset by this fact.

Realizing the other bears had taken the dead body away he knew trouble was ahead. He was sure it would not be long before more bears came knocking on their door. The most likely attack would come from the parlor door. Because of this he and Hugh sat in the parlor. Charles had the rifle and Hugh a pistol. In the kitchen Tony was holding the rifle and Margaret a pistol. Riley was with them with the bear spray.

Meanwhile Phoebe, with a can of bear spray in hand, sat in the dome car watching. She could easily come down the steps in case of attack. They stood on alert for over two hours. They were just beginning to think there would not be an attack when they heard Phoebe yell, "Here they come. There are two running towards the parlor and one towards the kitchen door."

Tony unlocked the kitchen door waiting. As soon as they saw the bear, he and Margaret began shooting. Somehow Riley was able to shoot the bear spray between them. The bear fell backwards and rolled off the train just like the one the night before.

Meanwhile Charles and Hugh stepped out on the platform and waited until the bears were close before they started shooting. The first one fell backwards but the other kept coming. He was trying to climb up on the platform. Just as he reached for Hugh's leg Phoebe, who was sitting on the floor, sprayed the bear's eyes.

Yelping with pain he fell back as the bullets finally hit an artery. All three bears lay next to the track dead. Charles was the first to yell out a cheer. He knew no more bears would attack. In fact, he saw two more down by the river start running towards the mountains. They sensed they could not win against this firepower.

It was hard to believe but it was over. They had beaten the bears. Just then they heard a loud noise overhead. A helicopter was coming into sight. All six of them were outside the train yelling and waving their arms. It looked as though they would finally be rescued.

The helicopter was able to land and the pilot came over to talk to them. He could not believe they had not been reported missing. The problem was the crewmen had assumed the bus driver had reported the train status. However, on one of his runs to the hospital that night the bus had gone off the road during an aftershock. The driver, while not dead, had been severely injured and had been on pain medication ever sense. He had totally forgotten about them.

As the helicopter was taking off Tony turned to Riley and kissed her. Without thinking Hugh did the same to Phoebe. It just seemed the natural thing to do. But, as they came apart, he was horrified by what he had done. "Oh, Phoebe, I am so sorry. I did not mean to do that. I guess I got caught up in the moment."

Nodding at him Phoebe stepped back. She had wanted the kiss to go on. She was not upset he had done it. How could she feel this way after what she had gone though with her husband; she did not know. All she knew was she would not mind being encircled in his arms forever. Maybe she was overreacting to last night and this morning.

They packed up their belongings, as they waited for the helicopter to pick them up. It could only hold three passengers at a time, but within two hours they were all safe and sound in the Whitefish hospital. They were feeling fine, but it was standard procedure to be checked out after such an ordeal.

As soon as Phoebe got to the hospital the message on her cell came to life. It was then she learned about her Aunt Phoebe and Uncle Henry. After talking to the nurse in charge of her aunt and uncle she went back and told the others what had happened.

She had tears in her eyes, as she talked about their passing. But knowing how much they loved each other she was glad they were still together even in death.

Hugh was deeply affected by Phoebe's story. If he had not seen it with his own eyes, he would not believe a couple could be so much in love for that many years. It really made him think about his own life. He was still upset that he had kissed Phoebe. He did not know what had come over him. He was usually very in control of his emotions.

He would need to think about what happened later. Right now it was just good to know they had been rescued. He had no idea his friend, Tony, was also wondering why he had kissed Riley.

Luckily, the Pullman had not been damaged. It took a couple of months to clear the track going east. Going west was another story. A trestle would have to be built over the chasm.   A helicopter was dispatched to collect their belongings which they had packed and left in the parlor. They stayed in Whitefish another two days. Phoebe had her aunt and uncle cremated, and then they all flew back to Chicago with the remains.

Phoebe and Riley were both thinking their psychologist was never going to believe what happened to them on their journey.

Chapter 34

It was three days after their return, on a Thursday, and Phoebe and Riley were meeting for lunch. Since Julia and Henry had a lot of friends, Phoebe had planned a memorial service on the following Saturday. She had emailed everyone she knew, whom she thought would like to attend, and also placed a notification in their local newspaper.

She was sad her aunt and uncle were gone, but she knew they would be happy that they were not apart. She had the funeral parlor place their remains together in the same urn and had them entombed in a crypt in a mausoleum in their home town. They had grown up in that town and had spent their whole married life there, so it seemed the appropriate thing to do.

She wanted the service to celebrate their life. Their lawyer called and told her she was the sole beneficiary except for college funds they had set up for Phoebe's grandchildren. They weren't what you would call extremely wealthy but they were very comfortable. It would take a year to settle their estate. But because of their advancing years they had planned out everything for their final demise.

In their later years they had volunteered helping

children. Phoebe wanted to find a way to put their money to good use in that direction. She had time to come up with some ideas, since it would be a year before she would receive all of the estate money.

Meanwhile she needed to go through their home and get the place ready for sale. She wanted to donate as much as she could, especially the furniture, to a battered woman's resale shop. She definitely had her work cut out for her in the next few weeks.

As she and Riley had guessed, the psychiatrist could not believe what an adventure they had. But he was more interested in the fact that they had found men to date and perhaps have a serious relationship with in the future. He thought both women were ready for this.

Riley was gushing with excitement over Tony. She told her friend that they had gone out the previous evening.

"Phoebe, you will never guess what he said last night." Not bothering to wait for a response she went on. "He told me he had really enjoyed being with me and working together on our trip. We had talked a little on the train about his past relationship. He decided it was time for him to see if dating someone seriously would lead to anything. After what we went through on the train, I was the only one he wanted to be with."

"Do you think you are ready to have a serious relationship?"

"I told him I am not sure if it will work out or not. But I wanted to give it a try. I talked to our doctor this morning and he said I was ready. His exact words were 'Life is so short you need to take a chance when it is offered. If it does not work out then so be it.' So I decided if I do not at least try it will definitely not work out."

Riley was beaming as she told her friend this. Phoebe had a feeling things would work out just fine for the two of them. As to herself that was a totally different matter. She still was not sure about dating again, but if she did she knew Hugh was the right man. But was he interested? That kiss said he was, but then he backed off so quickly she wasn't sure he meant to kiss her. It had probably just been a spur of the moment action from the excitement of being rescued. Only time would tell.

Riley was going out on a date with Tony Friday night. Then all four of them would meet up again at the Memorial service on Saturday. Perhaps she needed to speak to the doctor to see what he said about her having a romance. But that could wait until next week. Right now she was busy enough with the funeral preparations.

Her daughter and family were flying in for the service. She was really looking forward to spending the weekend with them. She would pick them up at O'Hare tomorrow at 2:00 p.m. On Saturday after the service she wanted them to go to Julia and Henry's home to pick out anything they wanted to keep in remembrance of them.

Once again Hugh interrupted her thoughts. Presently it seemed odd to even be thinking about him, but she had come a long ways in her new outlook. Before the train trip she would not have given having a romance a second thought. She had met quite a few men who had lost their wives to Alzheimer's at her lectures. They had made overtures towards her, but she had ignored them. She knew they were lonely men looking for companionship, but she liked her life just the way it was.

She knew her emotions got a little tangled up when she thought about Hugh. She had felt sensations she had not felt in a long time when they were on the train together. She kept trying to ignore the feelings. But after he had kissed her, she really started to wonder if she should let herself go and enjoy a relationship with him.

Obviously she needed to wait and see what he wanted to do about the situation. If he wanted to date to see if anything would come of things, she was willing to try. But if not, she would continue with her life the way it was. She enjoyed speaking to her groups and helping people get through their trying times with loved ones. Maybe that was what her mission for the rest of her life was all about.

Chapter 35

It was 3:00 p.m. and standing by the luggage carousel at O'Hare Phoebe saw her grandchildren come running towards her. Her daughter, Laura, and Pete, her husband, were right behind them. She could not believe how big they were getting. Time sure went fast as you aged she thought.

Jared, the oldest had just turned fourteen and Sara was twelve. They had always been very happy children and easy to deal with. She knew it was wrong, but she was glad that Dan was gone since he would never have gotten better.

She hoped time would erase all those sad visits they had with him when their grandfather was still alive. With any luck they would remember the kindness he showed them before his disease took its toll. She knew her daughter was trying to reinforce what a good man he had been in his lifetime.

They stopped at a favorite lunch place of Laura's, since it was only a little after 1:00 p.m. their time.

"You know, Mom, I love coming to see you. But it is also fun to come back and eat at some of my favorite restaurants here in the city."

"I know, dear, and that is why the kids and I are having pizza tonight while you and Pete go downtown to wherever you want."

Looking at her husband with a smile Laura said, "Thanks, Mom. We appreciate you letting us go out."

"I know you are on Los Angeles time but don't stay out all night. We need to leave tomorrow at 9:30 a.m. The service is at 10:30 a.m. followed by lunch in the church hall. I know lunch in the church basement does not sound very special. However Aunt Julia told me what kind of funeral arrangements she wanted, so I am just following her wishes."

The rest of the afternoon and evening went quickly. Before they knew it they were in the car the next morning headed for the church. The family stood in the vestibule at the back of the church and welcomed everyone.

Phoebe knew there would be quite a few people but she was amazed at how many actually came. Obviously her aunt and uncle were well loved. Luckily the church ladies who were doing lunch had an idea of how many people would show up and had plenty of food for everyone. Afterwards she gave them a large donation towards the food they had provided.

She introduced her family to Riley, Hugh and Tony who had come together. She really did not have time to visit with them, since so many people wanted to talk to her. She did make a lunch date with Riley for Tuesday.

She was shocked when she was standing alone for a minute, and Hugh came over and asked her to dinner on the following Wednesday night. He told her he had something important to ask her. Naturally she was taken by surprise, but agreed she would go out with him.

After the service she took her family over to Julia and Henry's house. Everyone picked out something they wanted to remember the couple by. A few of the items were a little bigger than they could put in their suitcase, so she promised she would ship everything to their home.

That evening they ate some leftover food the church ladies insisted they take. The next morning they had brunch at another favorite restaurant of Laura's. All too soon she was waving goodbye to them at the airport. She wished she lived closer to her family, but for the present her life was right here in Chicago.

She was sad when she got back home. The place seemed so silent with everyone gone. She decided she needed to call Riley with her news.

"Hi, Riley. The kids are gone and the place is so quiet I thought I would give you a call. You will never guess what happened yesterday at the church."

"I hope it is something good," her friend answered.

"Hugh asked me out to dinner Wednesday night."

"I thought you weren't interested in dating."

"I guess I have mixed feelings. I think I am open to something happening but at the same time, if it doesn't then that is okay too." Then she told her friend about Hugh's kiss.

"Wow! That is amazing. According to Tony, Hugh does not get that close to any women. I know when I went out with him it was strictly platonic. That was the way I also wanted it."

The two women chatted a little longer about the service and promised to meet on Tuesday for lunch. Since Riley was going out with Tony tomorrow night, she thought maybe she could find something out before their lunch.

They hung up and Phoebe took a bath and went to bed early. Because of her family's time difference, she had been up late the last two nights and was tired.

Chapter 36

Before she knew it Tuesday had arrived and it was time for her lunch date with Riley. Her friend seemed so happy and was gushing about Tony. Phoebe hoped she was not moving too fast into a relationship with him.

They had a few months to get to know each other due to the train trip but that had been on a casual basis. She worried they might be getting too serious too quickly after conditions had become so emotional during the earthquake. They had survived a scary ordeal and needed some time to really get to know one another.

"I know you think I am getting excited a little too quickly, but I really am not. I am still holding back. It is just that I haven't felt this way about someone for quite awhile and I am enjoying the feeling again. But I will be careful before committing my heart to him."

"I am happy to hear you say that, Riley. So did Tony mention anything about Hugh and me?"

"The other day at the memorial I mentioned how you wanted to honor your aunt and uncle with their money. You weren't sure what you wanted to do, but you wanted to do something for children. Tony did not say a lot, but he did say Hugh and his friend, who donated the house for the foster children, were cooking up a new deal. Maybe that is what he wants to talk to you about."

Greatly relieved that it probably was not about a relationship she told Riley she would call her on Thursday with a report. Meanwhile Riley was going out again with Tony on Wednesday night so maybe she would both learn more.

Hugh was at her door right at 7:00 p.m. as promised. She was all ready.

"What about Greek food? I know you mentioned you would like some when we were on the train."

That is perfect, Hugh. I have not had a chance to get to that restaurant since my return."

They both ordered gyros dinners and sipped wine, as they waited for their meals. Hugh said, "This is a little embarrassing but I want to clear the air between us."

Phoebe looked at him with a puzzled expression as he continued.

"When I kissed you I was shocked. You know I have not been interested in having a serious relationship with anyone and I know you do not want one either. At first I attributed it to the intense feelings we were having being rescued."

Just as I guessed, she thought.

He continued, "I kept thinking about why I did it. I

have not had a desire to kiss anyone in the last few years. I did not want to lead anyone on and it seemed the proper way to behave. However, we really got to know each other pretty well on that trip and I wondered if subconsciously I really did want to kiss you. I guess what I am trying to say is I have decided I am open to dating you and seeing where it will lead, if you are. I can't promise anything but I have a feeling you don't want to promise anything either. But, if nothing else, I think we can be great friends."

Phoebe totally taken aback by his declaration said, "I was also shocked when you kissed me. But I have to admit that I liked being kissed by you. Lately I have wondered if maybe I haven't totally shut myself off from having a relationship. I think I would like dating you just to see where the situation might lead. I don't think either of us is likely to cling, if one of us decides to end it."

At that moment their food arrived and feeling comfortable again with each other they started chatting.

"By the way I have something else I want to talk with you about. It is because of you that I have awakened to a new love of train travel. What I am about to tell you is a little sketchy in my mind right now. We would definitely have to work out the details. I want you to know Tony is having dinner with Riley tonight and talking to her about it, too."

Phoebe listened, as he continued.

"You know I have a friend who donated a mansion here in Chicago to use as a foster home for children where Tony and I help out. We use it as a temporary place until foster families can be found. However there are a few kids who live there permanently."

She nodded as he continued, "My friend, Adam, recently bought a place in northern Minnesota. He wants to turn it into a camp where foster kids can go in the summer to learn how to swim, fish, canoe, and horseback ride. When he opens it he will initially run it for five or six weeks, but eventually he wants to get it running for eight weeks every summer. In that way eight groups of foster kids would get a chance to spend a week there."

"That sounds like a terrific idea, Hugh."

"I think so, too. Here is the part where we come in. He had another friend who recently died. He had been restoring an old train car. He was only partly finished. His goal was to make it a sleeper car. When it was built it was known as a 10-6 sleeper meaning that it had 10 roomettes and 6 double bedrooms. The bedrooms have a toilet and a sink. The roomettes have a sink with toilets down the hall. The only significant modification to the interior that he made so far was to make one of the roomettes into a shower/changing room and another roomette into a galley, which would be used for microwaving snacks and serving hot and cold beverages."

"That sounds awesome, but why are you telling me about it?"

"His son is wealthy, in his own right, and is willing to sell us the car for one hundred dollars. He could use the tax right off against his father's estate. But there is still quite a bit of work to be done. Some of the work can be done by us and volunteers but we also have to hire out the train restoration work. That will be the big cost. Then, of course, there is the expense of maintaining the car. Our idea is to hook up the car to Amtrak for an overnight to Minnesota. We would take one group of kids up on a Saturday afternoon with an overnight stay on the train. And then the group already there would return to Chicago on Sunday morning."

Taking a drink of wine he resumed. "To be honest we need investors. Tony and I are putting money in. Riley mentioned you might be looking for something to invest your aunt and uncle's money in, if it helps kids. If you did this, we would happily name the car the J & H Camp Car in honor of them."

"Hugh, even if things don't work out between us, I think that is an awesome idea. I was talking to the lawyer yesterday and he said some money could be distributed early. I think my aunt and uncle would be thrilled about this. She told me in Glacier how much the train trip meant to the two of them. She knew their traveling days were numbered, and she was so happy the train was one of their last great adventures."

"I know you are busy with your speaking engagements, but besides putting money into the project we could use your help with the restoration. Adam, will also need help at the camp, too. He would like to have it ready so we could take the first group there towards the end of June next summer. He probably would keep running it through either the first or second week of August. That would give us a few weeks to see if there are bugs that need to be worked out."

"Are you talking about bugs both literally as well as figuratively?" she asked laughing.

"You are right," he said laughing with her. At least it

will give us time to see if a relationship between us will go anywhere."

"Don't worry about my speaking schedule. I can do as little or as much as I want. I usually schedule a month in advance, so it will be easy to cut back a little if I want to spend more time on your project."

"That is excellent. I hope Riley agrees to pitch in, too. It would be fun to have the four of us working together on this project."

"I think she will love to be involved, too. I don't know how much money, if any, she would want to give. But I do know she has been looking for something to occupy her days. She said she likes the idea of volunteering like you and Tony do."

"That settles it. Why don't we all go out to dinner Saturday night? I am sure Tony and Riley will be up for it. We can talk more about things then. Adam will be at the foster home on Friday afternoon. I will run everything by him, and let everyone know what his thoughts are."

It was almost 11:00 p.m. when they left the restaurant. "I don't know what happens when I go out to eat with you, Phoebe. It seems whenever we go to a restaurant we end up spending hours talking."

As he pulled up to her place she smiled at him. "Don't bother walking me to the door. I am fine. Why don't you call on Saturday morning to let me know what time we are going out. I will see you then. Good night, Hugh."

"Good night, Phoebe. See you on Saturday."

As soon as she went into her home, he drove off.

He had not kissed her goodbye. They were both still more comfortable at that point to keeping things casual. Only time would tell if they developed a more serious relationship.

Chapter 37

The two friends were on the phone with each other early the next morning.

"What did you think about the train proposal, Riley?"

"I think it sounds wonderful. I told Tony I would also like to help out with the camp next year. What a great opportunity for the foster children."

"It really is an excellent chance for them."

"I know they are in the beginning stages of putting everything together, but Tony said besides the train Adam will need help setting up the camp. He is thinking about having theme weeks to begin with. Once they decide which kids will be attending, he would give them a short survey on their likes and dislikes to help decide which week they might like best."

"What do you mean by themes, Riley?"

"There would be five or six sessions of camp offered the first year. All of the weeks would include traditional camp programming, but also have a specialized theme. They would include things like Adventure Week which would include rock climbing, caving and outdoor skills. Life Campers week would have an emphasis on fitness and healthy living. Splash and Sports week would concentrate on fishing and lots of water activities. They believe the Life Campers week would be especially good for overweight kids. They are also thinking of having a week for special needs kids. The following year, if all goes well, they would include horsemanship and a horseback riding option."

"Wow that is really a big undertaking. How many children would attend? I know Hugh mentioned eight roomettes and six doubles on the train."

"The eight roomettes will have bunks so they will sleep sixteen. One or two of the doubles will have adult chaperones. That leaves a minimum of four doubles. If we put two beds in each of the doubles, like Tony and Hugh had on the Pullman, we could easily take twenty-four to twenty-six children a week."

"That's incredible. Almost one hundred and fifty kids going to camp would be a tremendous start, Phoebe said."

"We would also look for some teens who would like to spend the summer there as camp counselors. We could even pay them a little. They would need training and everyone will be screened and monitored. We do not want any chance of problems or abuse to occur. Adam knows some teachers who could use extra money and were camp counselors when they were teenagers. He would hire them to set up the different programs."

"Now I know why Hugh said everything is in the planning stages. I can see there really are a lot of details to work out."

"The prospect of this whole concept really excites me, Phoebe. You know I never had children, and that fact did not really bother me. However, this project would give me a chance to help influence some kids in a positive way who might not otherwise get a chance to do something like this. I can picture myself spending six to eight weeks every summer at that camp helping out, and even riding the train back and forth each week."

"You certainly chose a worthwhile goal. I know Julia and Henry would be thrilled their money was going for such a meaningful project. Actually, I think helping with the train restoration would also be fun and would give me a chance to get to know Hugh a little better."

"I still find it hard to believe he is ready to consider a relationship with someone. But since he is, I am really happy it is with you."

"Well, time will tell. If we just end up being friends that will be fine, too."

Riley had a feeling that just being friends would not work out. She sensed they both liked each other. With her new feelings towards Tony, she knew Phoebe would enjoy a similar experience with Hugh. She also hoped that if the relationship did not work out, it would not threaten the outcome of their project.

Riley realized she was ready to commit to a new relationship. Both she and Tony had waited a long time to find someone whose company they enjoyed. She still did not think she wanted to get married again, but she could picture spending the rest of her life with him. It seemed they took pleasure in each other's company and there had been a couple of times they had even finished sentences for one another.

Riley had learned to enjoy being alone, but she also missed the companionship a relationship afforded. For the present the key was to get to know each other better, but keep their separate residences. Maybe something would happen and things would not work out, but she doubted it. Tony had waited a long time to find someone he wanted to be with and she had a feeling it would only get better.

He was so thoughtful. Her husband had been that way, too. But Jake had been so busy working that they never had a lot of time to play together. Since Tony was retired, he could spend as much or as little time as needed on his volunteer work. And that was enjoyable work. She had the feeling the next few months with the train and camp projects they would be very busy. However it would be very pleasurable work. She was certainly looking forward to the experience.

Hopefully Phoebe would also have a lot of fun with the projects. She had been through so much. Her speaking engagements had been a good way for her to work through her grief but she had closed herself off from the world. Her friend needed to start feeling again. It was difficult to open yourself up, especially when you feared failure, but it was time for her to move on to the next phase of her life.

Chapter 38

The four friends had gone out together on Saturday night to dinner and had talked most of the evening about their project. They met with Adam and his people the following Tuesday. Everyone was excited about what they were planning to do.

Adam really liked the train idea. It would be so much more fun and enriching than driving the children by bus to the camp. And it would really add to their experience. The property he had bought had a large house with a barn and was adjacent to a lake. There were over one thousand acres and he could picture riding paths and hiking trails all over the property.

The house itself was two stories with an attic and a basement. The upstairs had four bedrooms which could be used by the teachers or any adults they hired for summer help. The attic would be converted into two bedrooms and a sitting room. Adam would use one bedroom in the attic and any of his friends who wanted to help on various weeks could stay in the other one. The downstairs was typical with a living room, dining room, den or library and a kitchen. There was also a bedroom with a sitting area off the kitchen. The basement would eventually be set up as a workshop.

They would be building four outbuildings and one cabin. Three of the structures would be like a duplex with a wall down the middle. Each side would contain eight beds and a bathroom with four toilets and four showers. Everyone would have a built in dresser next to their bed for his or her belongings. One building could hold up to sixteen girls and one building sixteen boys.

The third building would have six beds with three bathrooms on each side for the camp counselors. One side would be for the girls and the other side for the boys. The fourth building would be the mess hall with a large kitchen. It would also double as a recreation area when the weather was bad and would contain a stage for programs.

There would be a cabin right next to the residence buildings. It would have a small sitting area, a bedroom and a bathroom. An adult couple would live there while camp was in session to oversee the dorms and be close in case of an emergency. There would be an intercom system between the cabin and the dorms.

"I want to provide a safe, fun, and small group environment which develops the spirit, mind, and body of each of the children. To me this camp will be a special place where the kids can learn about the environment, develop positive values, and make meaningful friendships. They will also learn new skills and increase their self-confidence," Adam told the others.

He continued, "These are kids without any families. I want them to learn that the friends they meet here can help them grow in a family like environment. And my hope is that the younger ones will grow up and become camp counselors themselves."

Everyone nodded as he continued.

"I have my people here working on setting up a charitable foundation. We are thinking of holding an auction once a year to help fund the camp. I have some influential friends who may be willing to speak at the auction. That should draw people in. Whenever I start a project like this many of my friends are only too willing to help. Some of them are always looking for tax write offs."

Then he continued, "We will also look at possibly getting some grant money. I just want this whole thing set up so if something happens to me the camp will continue to have the funding to go on."

"That is important," Hugh said. "Once it is up and running I know the children will look forward to going each year. As they get older, they will learn new skills and it would be awesome if they eventually became camp counselors. What a great way to teach responsibility and giving back."

"I agree, Hugh. I also need any help you four can give me with the camp property. Jared had most of the restoration completed. I assume you will have Avalon Rail in Milwaukee finish up the restoration on the sleeper. I know you will have some work to do with the sleeper. You will need to make decisions on ordering sheets, towels and window treatments as well as overseeing the work that is being done at the restoration company."

"I still don't know everything we will have to do with the restoration, but the four of us are going up to Milwaukee on Friday to meet with the sales person at Avalon. But what kind of help, Adam, do you need from us for your project?"

"I have some people working right now on the attic in the house to get the two bedrooms all set up. The sitting room will have a couch and chairs with a TV. There will be a desk with a computer and WiFi. I want it to be cozy and comfortable. Hugh and Tony, I have always trusted your judgment."

The two men smiled at their friend.

"I was hoping you and Phoebe and Riley would go up there for a week at a time twice a month. It is a good ten hour drive, if not a little more. It will take you a day to get up there and a day to get back. I would love it if you four would be in charge of ordering all the furniture, bedding, making the decision on the color of paint, and whatever else needs to be done. Eventually, I want King-size beds in the attic bedrooms, but you could put twin beds in for the present. We can always move the twin beds to the second floor later. Do you think you can do this for me?"

"We need to get together to see what kind of a schedule we can work out. Phoebe has her Alzheimer's speaking engagements to work around, but I am sure we can take care of this for you. Even though we would be working on this project, going to the north woods at this time of the year would be enjoyable," Hugh said.

"You would have carte blanche. All the decisions you make will be fine with me. You can just send the bills to my accountants. I have some other friends who are willing to go the opposite weeks when you are not there. They would oversee the painting and whatever else you set up, but I want you two men in charge of purchasing everything."

Not long after that the meeting ended. The couples

decided to meet for dinner the following night to talk over the proposal. After they dropped the women at their homes Tony said, "I was not really looking for this much work, but this is such a worthy cause. Adam has such a high opinion of our abilities I don't want to let him down."

"I agree with you. Even if the women are not on board I think we need to do it. But I would rather have the women with us. They would obviously be a big help."

"I am pretty sure Riley will go along. She is looking for something worthwhile to do. This would be a great way for us to spend time getting to know each other better to see if our relationship will go anywhere."

"Maybe Phoebe will feel the same way. I guess time will tell."

Before they knew it they were picking up the women for dinner. When they got to the restaurant they ordered wine and told the waiter they would wait awhile before ordering.

After their drinks arrived Hugh immediately said, "Well, what do you two think of Adam's proposal?"

Riley spoke first. "I want you to know that we called each other and talked everything over this morning. I am definitely in. I want to make a difference to children. I love this whole camp idea. I am willing to do whatever is needed to help make it happen." Looking at Tony she added, "And it will give us a chance to get to know each other better. Maybe our compatibility on the train was a fluke and maybe not. Doing this project will help us find out."

The three of them then turned to Phoebe. "I guess it is my turn," she said. "I am also willing to help. I don't have any speaking assignments the month of August because that is usually vacation time. I think if we plan to go the first and third weekends of each month, I could schedule my speaking around that in the fall. I cannot promise I will stick with it, but I want to try for a couple of months."

"That would be awesome, Phoebe."

"Thanks, Hugh. But I still want to be involved with the sleeper restoration, so we need to schedule our meetings when we are not up north."

"I agree. Since next week is the last week of July that will give us about ten days to plan before our trip. Tony and I will talk to Adam tomorrow and tell him our plans. That way he can get the ball rolling with the other people. Friday we can talk some more when we go to Milwaukee. Riley and Tony, do you want to go with us on Friday?"

As Tony nodded his head "yes" Riley said, "I was hoping you would ask us to go along. I am excited to see the sleeper."

"Then it's settled. We will pick you up Friday morning at 9:00 a.m. Do you mind going to Phoebe's house, Riley?"

"Sure that would be fine."

"Great now let's order dinner. I am starved."

Chapter 39

The sun was shining brightly at 9:00 a.m. sharp when Hugh pulled up to Phoebe's house. Their meeting in Milwaukee was scheduled for 11:00 a.m. It would take them about an hour and a half to drive there. They wanted some extra time in case they ran into traffic. They figured they could stop and get a cup of coffee and go to the bathroom, if they needed to kill time.

"Adam was so pleased the four of us are going to help him. He has men painting the attic this next week and one of his assistants ordered four twin beds and dressers for the bedrooms. He also ordered all the furniture for the sitting room. Since Adam plans to use one of the bedrooms he wanted the sitting room to have good quality furniture. He is having satellite television and WiFi installed next week, too. So we will have all the comforts of home."

At 10:55 a.m. they were shaking hands with the sales person at Avalon.

"I have to tell you I am not sure what amount Jared's family is selling the sleeper to you for but you are getting an excellent car. Most of the restoration is finished and paid for.

Hugh looked at Phoebe with a smile when he heard that.

"Let's go take a look at your car and I will explain what we have done."

They followed the salesman through the yard and across some tracks. They saw several cars being worked on.

"Here is what we have done so far. We have updated, and are working on, the interior including new wall coverings, carpet, window glazing and toilets all of which flush into holding tanks. All the furniture we have in the rooms came with the car. As you are probably aware, sleeper furniture is specialized in that the movable chairs fold. Fixed chairs and sofas likewise fold to reveal the beds when lowered for the night. And of course, all the beds are single or military twin."

"You don't have sheets or towels or any of that kind of stuff yet, do you?"

"No. Once we are close to finishing the restoration you can order all of those things. You will also need to buy new mattresses. We can recommend a couple of companies you may want to order from. Jared already picked out and paid for all the fabric for the chairs and sofas. We have the double rooms completed and are half way through the single rooms, as you will see when we walk through."

Hugh and Phoebe were both thinking that they were in much better shape as far as restoration than they first believed.

"As to the plumbing, the sinks and faucets are original to the car. They are stainless steel and fold up to drain and stow. The two rooms that are not original are the two roomettes we have repurposed. One will be used as a shower/changing room. It has a stall shower with a fixed head, a toilet and a sink. That room is also finished. But the other roomette is being made into a small kitchen that can provide food service for crew and beverage service for all. It will have a 4-burner electric cook top, microwave, refrigerator with freezer and a sink. That room still has to be completed."

"Do we need to buy those appliances?" Phoebe asked.

"Once again you are really lucky there. Just before Jared died, he ordered all the appliances and paid for them. They recently arrived. And the plumbing fixtures were found on some other train cars. He paid for them, and we restored them so they are like new. Another nice feature is the car has a circulating hot water system, so there is no wait for the water to get warm at the sinks anywhere in the car."

"What about the air conditioning and heat, "Hugh asked?

"The air conditioning system has been gone over several times in the life of the car, and it now has a diesel generator for standby power. All of the old electrical systems were removed and brought up to modern Amtrak standards. There is no longer steam heat in the car. Heat is accomplished via electric baseboards."

As he finished speaking he stopped in front of a car. "Well here it is. As I said, they are still working on it. But you will get a good idea how things are progressing."

At that point the five of them went up the stairs and walked the length of the car. They could really see the progress that had already been made and knew it would be perfect when completed.

"How much longer will it take you to finish?" Hugh asked the salesman.

"They are hoping to finish by Thanksgiving. Jared liked to come once a month to check on the progress. If you would like to do that it would be great. If you come sometime during the last week of each month, any issues that crop up we can get right on. I think, if everything goes according to plan, the last week in September you can order the mattresses. Then the last week in October you can order sheets, towels and kitchen supplies, including dishes."

"That sounds perfect," Hugh said. "We will be busy the first and third weeks of every month so the last week will work out well."

"Why don't you call me around the middle of August? We will set up a day that works best for you. I know you have a bit of a drive to get up here."

After they left Avalon they stopped downtown at a German restaurant that had been recommended to them before driving home.

"I almost forgot to tell you Adam has a friend who owns a motorcoach company. After a bus gets old and has too many miles on it they often sell them to Mexico or even Caribbean islands to use for tourism. He has one that is pretty old but is in very good mechanical condition. He plans to donate it to Adam. He is even having the seats refurbished."

"Why does he need a bus?" Riley asked.

"We need it to get the kids to and from the camp. It is a little less than a two hour drive from Minneapolis/St. Paul to the camp. The train gets into the Twin Cities about 10:30 p.m., if it is on time. I know the kids going to camp will be all excited and will not be sleeping well that first night. His thought is to put the children right on the bus that night and drive them to the camp. Even though they would get in late, they would be comfortable sleeping on the bus until they arrived at the dorms. They could sleep in a little on Sunday morning."

"That sounds like a good plan," Riley said.

"Yes it does. Meanwhile the kids who are finished with their week at camp would ride up on the bus that Saturday night and board the sleeper when it arrived. The train would be in position to couple the next morning and the kids would already be in their rooms. That way they would not have to get up at 4:00 or 5:00 a.m. to get on the bus to catch the train and would have an overnight in the sleeper. If the train arrived late at least they would be in their rooms on the Pullman sleeper and comfortable while they waited for the Empire Builder."

"That does make a lot of sense," Phoebe reiterated. "We could probably do KFC on the train going to camp and breakfast sandwiches and sub sandwiches on the journey home."

"I think we are getting ahead of ourselves dealing with the food," Tony said smiling. "For the present we have a house and several bunkhouses to get in order."

"I am really looking forward to that," said Riley as she shyly put her hand on top of his.

Chapter 40

It was 7:00 a.m. Sunday morning of the first week in August and Hugh and Tony had just picked up the two women.

Hugh was driving a minivan and Riley asked, "Where did you get this vehicle?"

"It is from Adam. He did not want me to use up a lot of miles on my car going back and forth to the camp every other week. He also thought a minivan would be good for hauling smaller supplies in."

"Well, it certainly is comfortable," Riley said from the seat behind the driver. The second row had two single seats with a space in between. The back seat had been folded down to make room for their luggage.

There were more bags than usual because the two men and Riley had packed clothes they could keep up at the camp. That way they did not have to pack a lot each time they came. Phoebe had also packed an extra bag, but not as big as she was not sure how many weeks she would be going up north.

Since they lived close to O'Hare they jumped on I-90 going west through Rockford and Madison, Wisconsin. In Madison they joined up with I-94 which took them all the way to Minnesota. It took eight hours to get to the Twin Cities which included lunch and gas stop.

Just east of St. Paul they caught I-35E going north so they did not have to go anywhere near the Twin Cities. They stopped to go to the bathroom and get a snack. Then they continued on their way. They had a little less than two hours to the Moose Lake region where the camp was located.

If they continued north another forty-five minutes, they would be in Duluth, Minnesota. Since the town had a population of over 100,000, they knew they would make a few trips there for needed supplies.

It was just after 5:00 p.m. when they arrived in Moose Lake. They still had about a fifteen minute drive to the property but not knowing the state of the kitchen they decided to eat dinner in town. They found a little café and were surprised at how tasty the food was. Then they stopped at a grocery store and picked up some food for breakfast in the morning.

They were tired from their journey but they knew this far north it would still be light out until at least 9:00 p.m. if not later. When they arrived at the house they were amazed at how pretty the property was. The home itself sat very near the lake and had a wrap-around porch that was screened in.

"Well that is definitely a good thing," Phoebe said. "I heard the mosquitoes here are extremely vicious especially at sunset."

"We need to put Off on our list; probably the deep woods kind," Phoebe added.

They started unpacking the car. When they got into the house the two men carried the suitcases to the third floor while the women put the groceries away before joining them. The two bedrooms were about the same in size and had bathrooms. Both rooms had windows overlooking the lake. The sitting room stretched across the back area of the house, and all the beds and furniture were in place.

There were new sheets still in packages with blankets and towels lying on their beds. Phoebe and Riley helped each other make their beds and put away their clothes and towels. Meanwhile the two men did the same in their room. It was almost 8:30 p.m. when they finished.

"Why don't we go downstairs, get a glass of wine, and sit on the porch to watch the sunset," Tony suggested.

They all agreed and headed down the stairs. After they got their wine they went to the porch. There was a loveseat, and Tony and Riley sat down together. There was also a swing with chains from the ceiling holding it up. Phoebe and Hugh sat in that. Since there was a slight breeze they could hear the waves lapping against the shore.

They sat there until after 10:00 pm. not saying much, but enjoying their first night in this magical place. They realized how awesome this camp would be for the foster children. They were happy they would be a part of putting this dream together.

They were up early the next morning and sat at the counter in the kitchen having breakfast.

"We do not have the bunkhouses to worry about right now. Adam has already had his people direct the workers on the paint that is to be used in the house. I think the first thing we must do is go through each room and make a list of furniture and whatever else will be needed. We should also include sheets, towels, and blankets on that list. Finally, we should purchase supplies like soap, shampoo and those kinds of items."

"You are right, Phoebe. We should get furniture in here quickly, especially a dining room table to eat on. We have to get everything in place, because Adam wants the bunkhouse builders to stay in the rooms on the second floor and eat in the house. When the workers arrive he plans to hire a housekeeper/cook who will cook, grocery shop and clean the bedrooms. The lady he has in mind is married. He thought her husband would be useful with helping his wife and taking care of any odd chores that need to be done."

"Since the two painters are coming every day from town we don't need to worry about them, but we need to order the furniture and pick out the carpet for the rooms. If the carpet people could do the measuring this week, then whomever Adam sends up next week can oversee the carpet being laid and the linoleum installed in the kitchen as the rooms get painted."

"We should probably use the company who laid the carpet up in our rooms," Riley said. "They certainly did a nice job."

Tony added, "When we come the next time if the floor covering and painting is finished we will have the furniture and appliances delivered. We can also get the sheets, towels, blankets, and whatever that week. That way we can have everything in the rooms before the workmen arrive."

Hugh then spoke up, "We also have to work on that room behind the kitchen. There is a bedroom and a sitting room back there. Adam said the couple can have that room. If we get those rooms finished they can move in when we come up the next time. I know it will be good to have others help with all of this work."

After breakfast they went though each room and made their lists. When the painters came they asked them to concentrate on the kitchen and the room behind it first. They called Adam's assistant and found out the carpet place was out of Duluth. They called the store and were reassured they had a large inventory. They would send two men first thing in the morning to measure.

After the men finished measuring the four of them would drive up to Duluth for lunch and talk to the flooring people. They knew they would be making another trip the following day to deal with the furniture. They also wanted to stop and get some groceries for the rest of the week. The refrigerator and stove weren't the greatest but at least they worked.

Feeling good about all they had accomplished they drove back into Moose Lake for lunch and bought a few groceries for dinner. The men had found a grill that was in good shape in the barn. They bought charcoal and fluid and after cleaning the grill they cooked steak and baked potatoes for dinner.

After dinner they sat on the porch and talked about all they had accomplished. With trips to Duluth the next two days they knew the week would go quickly.

Chapter 41

They were finishing their cereal and coffee the next morning at 8:30 a.m. when the doorbell rang. It was the flooring men.

Tony and Hugh took the men up to the third floor bathrooms so they could start measuring for tile while the women washed the dishes, since it was their turn. The four of them met on the second floor while the men were doing the bedrooms and bathrooms on that floor. After that the carpet men moved to the downstairs and did all the rooms there. It was almost 11:00 a.m. when they finished measuring and departed.

A few minutes later the four of them were headed to Duluth. Since they did not know how long they would be tied up at the flooring place, they decided to have lunch first. It was almost 1:00 p.m. when they arrived at the store. It took them over two hours to get everything picked out but they were happy with their choices and the owner of the shop made sure everything they had chosen was in stock. He set up the install for the following week.

They stopped at a large grocery store chain and bought food as well as cleaning and bathroom supplies. After such a busy day they also picked up dinner that they could zap in the microwave.

It was 6:00 p.m. by the time they got back to the house. They put everything away, had dinner and sat on the porch before going to bed. The next morning they were on the road by 9:00 a.m. headed back to Duluth to the furniture store.

They ordered everything they needed for the house including the appliances. As soon as they had the carpet and tile in place the store would deliver the furniture. As long as the flooring was installed the store promised everything would be in place by the end of the following week.

Feeling good about all they were accomplishing they spent the rest of the week cleaning the bathrooms and other odd jobs. In the afternoons they spent time walking the hiking trails and exploring the property. In the evening after dinner they sat on the porch talking. Each couple was really getting to know one another and all four of them enjoyed being together.

Before they knew it their week was over. A married couple, Julie and Jack, who were friends of Adam's were to stay at the camp on the opposite weeks and had arrived Saturday night. They were staying overnight at a local hotel, since there were no beds for them at the house. Hopefully that situation would be rectified by the following week.

They invited the couple over for dinner so they could go over everything that had been done and what they would need to do the upcoming week. They showed them all over the property and explained about the flooring and furniture.

The washer and dryer would not be installed until the end of the week after the flooring was in. Because of this they had bought extra sets of sheets and towels for the couple.

They planned to leave for Chicago at 8:00 a.m. They had given Julie and Jack a set of keys at dinner that night. The couple planned to have breakfast at the hotel and get to the camp by 9:00 a.m. There was not much for them to do on Sunday, but they would be busy once the work week started.

Going back to Chicago seemed almost surreal. They felt as if they had been living in a different world up at the camp and were looking forward to the following week when they went back up there. Riley and Tony were seeing each other every day. They both had been alone for awhile, especially Tony, and neither of them could believe how much they missed each other when they were apart.

Worried that the bubble would burst on their romance they decided to just enjoy each day with each other. If things did not work out at least they had these days together. Neither of them could believe how quickly they had become attached to each other.

Riley's psychiatrist told her that sometimes people know quickly that they are meant for each other. Especially considering their ages, it was not unusual to bond quickly. It scared them how they often finished each other's sentences, as if they had been together for a long time.

But for now they were having fun. Riley even went to help Tony at the foster home on Thursday and Friday. She thought it would be good to get to know some of the kids she would be dealing with at camp next summer and for them to be comfortable with her.

In the mean time while it was obvious there was a spark developing between Phoebe and Hugh, they were definitely proceeding more cautiously. They were both experiencing feelings they had not felt in years. The atmosphere between them was like a volcano that had been dormant for many years, but was slowly waking up.

Unlike Riley and Tony they were definitely taking things slow and easy. Being together at the camp was fun and they were learning to appreciate each other. However, back in Chicago they preferred their space. They did go to dinner Tuesday night, and they seemed to talk for hours after not seeing each other for two days.

Phoebe had a speaking engagement on Thursday, and Hugh was busy with the foster children both Thursday and Friday. All four of them were going to dinner Saturday night. They wanted to get an early start on Sunday morning so they decided not to stay out late.

Hugh came to Phoebe's door to pick her up. He rang her doorbell. When she opened the door, without thinking, he took her in his arms and kissed her. Surprised by his display of affection he said shyly, "I think I missed you."

"Well, if you want to do that again I would like it because when you kissed me I realized I missed you, too."

Kissing her again he said, "We had better get going, if we want to meet Tony and Riley. If we keep up the kissing, we might not make it to dinner."

For some reason that thought both scared her and excited her. She had not been out on a date since before she was married and she wasn't sure how to proceed with things. She almost felt maybe she should run away from this possible romance.

She wondered should they seize the moment which could lead to fulfilling each other or would they let this chance pass them by? She had the feeling even though he had just kissed her, that Hugh was also ambivalent. When the chips were down he might be skittish too. Well, I guess only time will tell she thought.

"We better hurry. I don't want Tony and Riley to have to wait for us," she said with a smile.

Chapter 42

It was Sunday, and once again they were headed north. They stopped for lunch in Eau Claire, Wisconsin which was a little over half way. They met Julie and Jack at a restaurant very near the interstate.

The couple filled them in on everything they had accomplished. The housekeeper and her husband would be arriving after lunch on Monday. Julie had made sure their rooms were all set for their arrival including making their beds.

The painting was finished by Tuesday. In addition, the flooring people had worked through the week and finished up late Thursday afternoon. Jack was excited for them to see how nice the carpet and tile looked. The new appliances and furniture had been delivered on Friday.

"All the appliances are set up and running. And we did several loads of wash." Julie added. "I washed all your sheets and towels. Jack helped me make your beds, so you have fresh linens when you get there. I know after this weekend the housekeeper will take care of that, but I did not want you to have to deal with bedding when you got there tonight."

"The bedroom furniture has been placed in the rooms on the second floor but you may want to rearrange some of it. They were working very late on Friday. In the last couple of bedrooms I had them just put the beds together and leave all the furniture in the middle of the room," Jack told them.

Adam's people had hired some local construction workers. In addition there were six workmen coming from out of town on Tuesday afternoon who would be staying in the house until the outbuildings were complete. There had also been some lumber and other supplies delivered and Jack had everything placed in the barn.

"I know there is no rain in the forecast, but I thought those items should probably be protected in the barn. Once the workers get there they can decide what goes where."

"That was great thinking," Hugh told Jack. "I hope you two have a great week off and we will meet again here next Sunday."

"Sounds good," the couple said at the same time as they all exited the restaurant to their vehicles.

They were excited and looking forward to their next week at camp. There would be a lot of things happening this week. When they got to the property it almost felt like they were driving in to their vacation home when they drove up the driveway and saw the house in front of them.

Julie had made a hotdish and put it in the refrigerator to surprise them. All they had to do was warm it up in the oven. They just had duffel bags with them since they had left a lot of things on their first stay. They took the bags up to their rooms and then walked through every room on each floor. They were amazed how wonderful everything looked and what a difference a week made.

They were tired from their long drive and decided to rest that evening. They would rearrange the bedroom furniture in the morning. The housekeeper and her husband, Irene and Jerry, would be arriving right after lunch. They planned to spend the afternoon showing them around and having them get settled in.

On Tuesday morning they would go to Duluth and get sheets and towels for the second floor bedrooms. They wanted Irene and Jerry to go with them, so they could get groceries for the week. There was a chain grocery store in Duluth, and Hugh had talked to the manager when they had stopped previously. He had agreed to set up an account that would be billed directly to Adam's office. A credit card would be placed on file to guarantee payment.

After they arrived back from Duluth Irene and Jerry would take care of the groceries and make dinner. Everyone else would help with making beds and getting the bathrooms ready for the arriving workmen.

It was 1:00 p.m. on Monday when the couple arrived. They liked them immediately and knew Adam's people had made a good choice. Irene told them how excited she and her husband were with the work. She and Jerry had recently retired and being able to spend their summers at the camp would be an ideal job for them. And they would be out of the heat of the city during the hot months.

This year they would work until the outbuildings were completed probably until the end of October or first of

November. Then everything would be closed up. Even the water would be turned off. An alarm system would be installed to keep the place safe during the winter months.

Jerry had been a janitor, and Irene had cooked for a large school district. They knew this would be the perfect job for them. Adam wanted them to come up two weeks before camp started to get everything in order, and stay two weeks after it was over to get everything closed down for the winter.

With the money they made in the summer, Irene and Jerry were planning on living somewhere in the south in the winter. They were even thinking if things went well they would rent out their home. Irene had a sister who had a finished basement with a bedroom, living room, and bath. They could rent that for the few months they would be back in Illinois.

Everything moved along without a hitch. The workmen arrived at 4:00 p.m. on Tuesday afternoon. Everyone met after breakfast on Wednesday, including the men from town. Hugh and Tony got good vibes from the workers especially, the foreman, Lou.

Adam wanted Irene to fix breakfast and lunch for everyone, including the men from town. He thought the crew might work more efficiently, if they were well fed and got to know each other. Naturally dinner was provided for anyone living in the house.

Irene would be busy with cooking and buying groceries for three meals a day. The weekly people would take care of the cleaning. Actually, now that everything was proceeding and well organized, there was not a lot for the four of them to do anyway.

Irene and Jerry planned to take care of their own rooms. The four of them decided they would also take care of their own rooms and bathrooms. They would divide the second floor in half. That way the work was pretty evenly distributed. Jerry was put in charge of vacuuming and cleaning the linoleum as well as helping Irene with whatever she needed.

Hugh and Tony told Lou that he was responsible for the work, and they would not be second guessing him. However if he needed any help with supplies or other issues, they would be there for him. He seemed a good natured man and was impressed that Jack had placed the materials in the barn.

Lou did not think it would be difficult to get the out buildings up within a month. Then they had another month to work on the inside when the weather turned cooler. They were installing bathroom fixtures and electric baseboard heaters, but the electrical work would not be finished until the following spring before camp opened. Even the flooring and beds would wait until spring.

Chapter 43

Except for the constant construction noise things went really well that week. The two couples spent a lot of time walking the property. In the evening they played cards, and sometimes some of the others joined them.

They made another trip to Duluth on Friday. Although they had their own vehicle, Irene and Jerry went with them. Irene needed more groceries, so they dropped the couple off while they went to a large sporting goods store.

Adam liked supporting the local economy whenever possible so they checked on canoes, life jackets and other items that would be needed for the camp. Over the next few weeks they planned to have all the furniture picked out for the outbuildings as well as the sheets, towels, and flooring. Then everything would get ordered and delivered in the spring when they opened the house once more.

They left on Sunday and had lunch with Julie and Jack in Eau Claire again. Before they knew it they were back in Chicago. Tuesday morning all four went together to check on the sleeper in Milwaukee. Little by little they could tell progress was being made.

They had lunch with Todd who was extremely excited about their sleeper. He had never had enough money to restore one himself. Besides the Pullman they had rented, Todd had another car. The main level had forty two reclining seats with tables for thirty six of his passengers. There was also seating for twenty four at tables in the vista dome. There was a wet bar and a full commercial kitchen.

He used the car for a lot of day trips, and once in awhile for an overnight if people were willing to sleep on a reclining seat. Since they would only use their sleeper car in the summer months, he thought he could perhaps use it other times of the year and attach it to his coach car. In return he would either rent it from them or let them use his Pullman whenever they wanted it, if he did not already have it rented. Naturally, the four of them were excited at the prospect of possibly touring in the Pullman again.

September and October flew by. Phoebe had one speaking assignment each month and picked the second week of the month. That way she was able to continue going to the camp with the others.

It was amazing how quickly the outbuildings had progressed. Adam had bought a prefab log cabin and that was already in place. The whole area was changing but it seemed for the better.

By the third week in October as much as possible had been completed for the year. It felt a little sad that everyone was leaving for the winter. The alarm system had been installed and Tony, Hugh and Jerry started closing everything down. The water was turned off after the women had washed all the sheets and towels and packed everything away for the winter.

It was almost noon on Friday when they drove away from the camp. There had been some snowflakes the day before and they knew winter was coming. Saying goodbye to Irene and Jack, the four of them wished them well with their winter plans. The couple had been to Florida previously, so this winter coming up they were going to try south Texas.

It was 10:00 p.m. before Hugh dropped the women at Phoebe's house. They would be going to Milwaukee the following Tuesday. The sleeper car was almost finished. They just needed to order their mattresses, linens and towels. The company promised everything would be finished before Thanksgiving. The dishes and towels they had picked out would have the J&H logo on them.

Todd had leased the sleeper car from them over the Christmas holidays, so it would already start generating an income. They planned to keep the sleeper in Wisconsin, because the cost of leasing space to store the sleeper was less than in Chicago.

As the start of the holiday season began everything regarding the camp was finished for the year. They had gotten a lot done. It was a good feeling. Adam was amazed at how much they had accomplished.

There was some other news, too. Riley and Tony had become engaged. Riley planned to rent out her house and move in with Tony. Her house had memories of her husband, while Ginger had never lived in Tony's present place. So it seemed the logical place for them to move in together.

Phoebe and Hugh's romance had been moving along

well, but not to the point of moving in with each other. At this point in their relationship they were both still too skittish for that. Everything seemed too good to be true. They would soon discover that it was.

Chapter 44

They had finished ordering everything they needed for the Pullman the week before. The company was putting the finishing touches on everything. They planned to take possession the following week.

It was the weekend, and they were out to dinner together. Riley and Tony were busy discussing their holiday plans.

"What are you two doing for the holidays?" Tony asked Phoebe.

"I am not sure what Hugh is doing," she said as she looked at him. "I am going to California for Thanksgiving and staying through Christmas. I spend the holidays with my daughter and her family every year. It is nice to get out of this cold weather."

Hugh looked surprised but did not say anything about her announcement.

"What about you, Hugh," Riley asked.

"I am not sure yet. Sometimes Adam goes off to some exotic location, and I tag along."

"Well that sounds like fun," Phoebe said to him.

Hugh nodded his head. Nothing more was said on the topic. During the next week and a half Phoebe noticed Hugh did not seem his usual cheery self.

"Is there something wrong, Hugh?" she asked him several times. He always shook his head "no."

He asked her to go out dinner with him the Monday night before Thanksgiving. Everything with the sleeper was finished and it was in storage waiting for Todd to use over the Christmas holidays. Phoebe was planning on flying to California first thing Wednesday morning. She was really excited to see her daughter and grandchildren again. She had not seen them since the funeral.

There was definitely something wrong! Hugh picked her up at the door as usual but he did not attempt to kiss her. She immediately got a bad feeling that she was not going to like what was coming. She decided not to say anything, and let things unfold as he wanted them to.

Pretending nothing was amiss, she got into the car. She ordered her glass of wine when the waiter came to the table but Hugh just asked for water. Knowing she could no longer ignore the situation she asked, "What's wrong Hugh? You have been acting strangely for the last couple of weeks."

"I don't know where to begin, Phoebe."

"Well, start some place."

"I hate doing this when Tony and Riley are so happy, but I don't think we should date anymore."

"Have you found someone else?"

"Oh heavens, no."

"After you said you were going away for the holidays I started thinking about things."

"What you don't want me to go visit my family?"

"I would never ask you to not visit them. It is just we have been floating along in this relationship, and we could easily keep doing it for a few more years. But the more I think things over, the more I realize I don't want to change my life. I don't want to get married, or move in with you or any of the things Tony and Riley are doing."

"I never asked you to do those things."

"I know you haven't. But eventually seeing how happy Tony and Riley are you might come to expect the same happiness. And you deserve it. I just can't provide it. Rather than getting more serious I think we need to cool down. I hope by next summer we can just be friends. But if you don't want that, I will respect your wishes."

She sat there while he talked just feeling numb. She did not even take a drink of her wine.

"I was thinking, if you are too upset with me over this, we could do opposite weeks at the camp next year. I want you to be able to be involved. I will even pay you back for all the money you put into the sleeper. It will take me a while, but I don't want you to think I was using you for your money."

"You do not need to pay me back anything, Hugh. That

was my aunt and uncle's money and it went for a cause they would be proud of. I just hope you will keep using their initials in memory of them."

"I would never change that, Phoebe."

"As to next summer I have no idea how I feel about that right now. The camp is yours and Adam's vision and I want you to be comfortable about being there whenever you want to go. I can stay busy with my Alzheimer's work."

"I just want you to know you would be welcome anytime. You did a lot of work up there this year to get the project off the ground."

"Hugh, I am not very hungry right now. I think I will take a cab home."

"No, let me drive you."

"I don't want you to drive me. A cab will be fine."

With that she got up and left the table. There were tears in her eyes when she left the restaurant, but she was too much in shock to even cry.

By the time she got home, she had almost convinced herself it was for the best. At least she would be gone for the next few weeks. If she had been home, too many things might remind her of him.

She had promised to meet Riley for lunch the next day. She thought of cancelling, but realized that would not be fair to her friend. Plus she did not want her to hear the news second hand.

Riley was shocked. She could not believe Hugh had broken up with her. "I know he has issues, but you were not demanding at all. Why he did not want to keep the relationship going the way it was is a mystery to me. I know you would never have pushed him to do something he did not want to do."

"I don't get it either. Maybe he felt he was getting more serious than he wanted, and being scared he decided it was better to end it sooner rather than later. At least going to my daughter's house I won't have much time to dwell on the situation."

"I certainly hope this will not affect our relationship."

"Well, obviously it will a little. I will still go out to lunch with you and would love to see you and Tony. But I do not want to be around you, if Hugh is there. I don't want him to think I am trying to get back together with him."

"I understand that, but we are talking about getting married next summer sometime and I want you as my matron of honor…Hugh or no Hugh."

"I am really honored you want me in your wedding. Frankly I would not miss it whether he is there or not. That is a long way off. I know I will be able to be around him for a couple of days at that point."

Riley had tears in her eyes when she hugged her friend goodbye. "Tony and I are going to the Caribbean for the New Years. But as soon as we get back I will call you, and we will meet for lunch.

"It's a date," Phoebe said smiling.

When she got in her car to drive home she turned on the radio and an old Barry Mani low tune was playing. She had always liked the song but she almost turned it off twice, because of the message. But in the end she let the song finish:

We had the right love at the wrong time

Guess I always knew inside

I would not have you for a long time.

Somewhere down the road

Our roads are going to cross again

It does not really matter when

But somewhere down the road

I know that heart of yours will come to see

That you belong with me.

How wrong those words were. Oh well I guess I just need to get on with my life. I was happy before Hugh and I can be happy after Hugh, too.

Chapter 45

Phoebe never told her daughter about Hugh. Normally Laura would realize there was something different about her mother, but she was so excited about the family being together for the next few weeks that she did not realize her mom was a little more subdued than usual.

It was hard to be too downcast with the children running around the house excited about the holidays. There were one or two friends over most of the time, so the house was always filled with children's voices.

That is one thing I will miss about not going to camp next year. I was really looking forward to working with the foster kids she thought. She did tell Laura how awesome the sleeper had turned out and about the J&H logo not only on the outside, but also on the dishes and towels.

"Mom it's really wonderful you were able to do that for Aunt Julie and Uncle Henry. I know they would be so happy to know their money was benefitting children. Now that you are finished with that project have you thought anymore about moving out here closer to us. There are a lot of places where you can do your speaking engagements and I know you will make friends easily. Abby is really looking forward to bumming around with you these next few weeks."

"I have always liked your mother-in-law. We have a lot in common. I was very sad when her friend, Tom, died last year."

"That was a sad time. I told her maybe she will find someone else to be with. But she said she has had two men whom she loved dearly and who loved her back. That was enough for a lifetime."

"If you don't mind me hanging around, I was thinking about staying until spring. I can do things with Abby and maybe even check out places I may want to live, if I move out here."

"Oh, Mom, that would be terrific. We would love having you."

Abby and Phoebe met the following week. They had decided they would shop and do the cooking for Thanksgiving. Since Laura worked, it would give her a break. They had a nice lunch while discussing what they would need to buy and cook.

"I am so glad you are here Phoebe. I am hoping you will join me a couple of times next week at my Senior Center. We play cards every Tuesday afternoon and there is always a speaker on Thursdays. Laura said you were thinking of staying until spring. We could have a lot of fun together."

"That sounds great, Abby. I don't want to wear out my welcome. Since Laura wants me to move out here, I thought I might look at properties while I am at it."

"There are always a couple of properties available where I live. You need to check that out first. I have always enjoyed your company Phoebe. I think we could have a lot of fun together."

"I do too, Abby."

I know Laura told you we are going to take that four day cruise between Christmas and the New Year. You and I will be rooming together. I have four other lady friends from the Senior Center who are also going. That will give you a chance to get to know some of my friends. And, since the kids are each bringing a friend, they will be busy."

"I always enjoy cruising. You unpack once and keep moving. Aren't we going to Catalina Island and Ensenada in Mexico?"

"Yes, nothing too exciting, but I like the shows and activities on board and naturally all the food."

"Laura told me all about your trip on the Pullman last summer. And she mentioned you were fixing up an old sleeper car with your aunt and uncle's money. But I have to say you just have not seemed your usual happy self since you came out here."

Phoebe told her friend about Hugh and breaking up with him. "You know, Abby, sometimes I am glad it is over and other times I am sad wondering what might have been."

"Let me tell you something very few people know. After Pete's father died I was alone for almost ten years. Pete was in college. I was secure financially, and quite frankly, I was not interested in another romance. Then I met Tom. We had an almost instant connection."

"I did not realize you were alone that many years."

"I was. But things were moving so fast that Tom, like your Hugh, decided we needed to call it quits. It is strange how my story sounds so similar to yours. Tom had a bad marriage. He could not believe things would continue as well as they were for an extended period of time. And, he said almost the same thing Hugh did. It was better to break it off immediately before someone got really hurt, if it ended later."

"That is amazing. I always wondered where does friendship end and love begin. But in your case what brought the two of you back together?"

"We met about three months later at a charity event. I probably would have ignored him, but he did not look well. I went over to him and asked him if he was sick. He broke down and told me the worst mistake he ever made was breaking up with me. I moved in with him the next day."

"I know you lived together for twelve years, but you never married."

"Neither one of us felt the need to get married. We just liked being together and we had twelve blissful years. We traveled all over the world and did everything together. I know how your Aunt Julia felt when Henry died. I felt the same way when Tom died. But somehow I kept living and the pain lessened. I have had two wonderful men in my life, but I do not want another one. All the happy memories keep me going."

As Phoebe nodded at her in understanding she continued, "But what about you? What are you going to do?"

"You know Laura is pushing me to move out here. I am not really opposed to that. I don't plan to chase after Hugh. If it is over, it's over. Yet somehow I feel I still have things to do back there. I want to go back and spend the summer in Chicago. I don't know if it is possible, but I would really like somehow to be involved with the camp. But I don't want to be there, if Hugh is there."

"Well as long as you are so ambivalent, I think the best thing for you to do is go back. You could always sell your house and move out here next fall. Weren't you planning to spend the winter here?"

"No, I was going home after the New Year, but now I don't plan to go back until sometime in March when the weather gets better there. There really is not anything for me to rush back to. I am planning to bum around with you the next four months, Abby."

"Wonderful. I know you will like my friends and we will have a good time together."

It turned into a really great winter. The holidays were fun. The cruise was amazing, although the biggest complaint from everyone was that it was too short. Phoebe and Abby settled into a routine of time spent at the Senior Center during the week. And, Phoebe spent her weekends with Laura, Pete and their children.

Phoebe had such a good time she began to wonder if she shouldn't just move to California after she sold her house. She missed Riley but other than that there was not much waiting for her back in Chicago.

As she wrestled with the dilemma, fate took over.

Chapter 46

It was the end of February and just as Phoebe was leaving for the Senior Center the telephone rang. It was Riley.

"Oh, Riley it is so good to hear your voice."

"And yours, too, Phoebe."

"You sound so happy. I guess you and Tony are still going strong."

"We are, and we're definitely planning to get married this summer. That is one of the reasons I am calling. I know I mentioned it before, but will you be my Matron of Honor?"

"I would love to. Thank you for asking me."

"That's wonderful. Now the second reason I am calling is about camp. I know you said you wanted to be involved this summer, but do you still feel that way?"

"I do, Riley, but I don't really want to be around Hugh."

Riley did not want to tell Phoebe how miserable Hugh had been since she left. He pretended he was happy.

But Tony knew his friend and realized he was extremely unhappy. Instead she said, "Well that is excellent. Hugh has been tied up with the financial end of the summer camp rather than anything related to the actual running of the camp."

She then continued, "He also has been busy renting the sleeper out. But the reason I am calling is because Adam's people are now setting up a committee to start working on activities and programs for when the children are at the camp. Tony and I are involved along with the teachers who plan to be summer camp counselors. We sure could use your help."

"That sounds exciting. When would you need me? You are sure I will not run into Hugh helping this way?"

"No, you won't run into him. And we could use you yesterday. How soon can you come?"

"Well today is Tuesday. I could probably get a flight home on the weekend. How about we set up a meeting for a week from today on next Tuesday?"

"Oh, that would be great, Phoebe. We probably could do an early dinner meeting since the teachers are working until about 4:00 p.m. Why don't you call me with your flight information and Tony and I will pick you up at the airport. We can stop and have dinner somewhere before taking you home since your cupboards will be bare."

"Okay. That works for me. I will email you as soon as I have the flight information."

After telling Laura her plans, her daughter was a little upset that she was leaving so quickly.

"Laura, this is something I really want to do. It is so exciting being in on the ground floor of this project. But I have been thinking about living out here. I think I will put the house up for sale this next summer and then move out here sometime in the fall. Even if I live here I will want to continue to help with the children. I could still go back to the camp every summer to help. There is plenty of space and if this grows, as I believe it will, they will need a lot of help."

"Oh, Mom, it would be so great if you moved out here. I know the kids would love having you here. Just the other day Pete was saying how happy he is you and his mother have become such good friends."

"If I do come out here next fall, I think I would like to move into that retirement village where Abby lives. Besides the Senior Center, there are a lot of activities where she lives, too."

The rest of the week passed quickly. In no time at all it was Saturday, and Laura and Pete were driving her to the airport. Her plane left at 11:00 a.m. and with the flight schedule and time change she touched down in Chicago just before 5:00 p.m. Riley and Tom had parked in the Cell Phone lot and as soon as she saw her luggage she called them. It was only a couple of minutes after she walked outside that they pulled up to get her.

She was so glad to see her friend. It was obvious Tony was very much in love with Riley. She did not know a man could glow, but they both seemed to. They stopped at a chain restaurant near the airport for dinner.

"So, when is the wedding?"

"We are getting married in June a couple of weeks before camp starts. We plan to take the children on the train the first week, and then spend the summer there. Adam wants us to move into the bedroom on the third floor that you and I stayed in last year. He plans to come up now and then but he said we won't bother him being in the room next door."

"So you are sharing your honeymoon with the foster kids," Phoebe said with a smile.

Blushing they both nodded "yes."

Then Riley continued, "But actually we have booked the Pullman for the first two weeks in September. That is a slow time for Todd. It has really helped his business being able to use the sleeper. So he is letting us use it for free. We will pay Charles and Margaret's salaries, food, and whatever Amtrak fees are involved. That will be our real honeymoon."

Tony spoke up, "We are not exactly sure of our itinerary yet. We thought we would take the Empire Builder to Glacier since we did not do that portion of the trip due to the earthquake. Then we might take the Coast Starlight down to Los Angeles to see the ocean views. From there we can take the Southwest Chief home." He did not tell her that Hugh was also going along.

"I think we have created a monster," Riley said laughing. "Tony is definitely hooked on long distance train travel."

After dinner they took her home and made sure she got in all right. Since it was March, Tony checked her heat because the outside temperature was only in the low 40s.

They planned to pick her up at 4:00 p.m. on Tuesday. They would meet the others on the committee at that time and have an early dinner.

As they left, Tony turned and said, "Riley told me you don't want to run into Hugh. I want you to know I do not blame you. Don't worry we will only see you when we are not with him. I won't even tell him you are back."

He could tell saying this to her was a great relief. However, it made him sad. He had loved Hugh like a brother all his life. He knew his friend had made a big mistake letting her go. But such was life. It was up to them to find their way back to each other if it was meant to be.

"Thank you, Tony. I really appreciate your thoughtfulness."

Chapter 47

Tuesday night was a lot of fun and very productive. The teachers were perfect for the assignment. One was a physical education teacher and his wife was a music teacher. The other was an art teacher and his wife taught Home Economics.

The two couples were friends outside of school and were looking forward to their summer in Minnesota. Not only would they be paid for their services, but they would be doing work they all loved. In addition, it would get them out of the heat of the city. They planned to go up the week before camp started to get everything prepared ahead of time.

"Wow," Phoebe remarked. "Adam could not have hired a more perfect complement of employees. You four will be amazing at putting together the perfect blend of programs and activities for the children."

"Thank you," they all said at the same time beaming. "I think that is why Adam hired us," Joanne the Home Ec teacher, said. "He liked our different backgrounds but he also liked the fact that we are friends. He felt we would be a much more effective team since we know and like each other."

They spent the next hour discussing what they thought would be some good programs to include. They agreed to meet once a week to work everything out and make lists of supplies that would need to be ordered. They planned to do some special activities on the different themed weeks.

Riley and Tony had already talked Phoebe into taking care of the children in the evenings. Instead of a couple, she would stay in the cabin next to the bunkhouses. That way she would have her own space. She was looking forward to spending her summer at camp, especially since her friends would be there.

She might not be able to avoid Hugh completely. He was not planning on spending the summer there but would come up on occasion. At least she did not stand the risk of running into him in the big house because she had her own cabin.

Phoebe decided she could live with those terms. She planned to go early when Irene and Jerry opened the house. She was in charge of getting all the furniture for the bunkhouses and her cabin set up; as well as ordering the linens, the towels, and whatever else needed to be done.

She realized even if Hugh did show up she could pretty much avoid him with all the duties she had. And so spring passed quickly. She did a few Alzheimer speeches, and went to lunch every Tuesday with Riley as they had done previously. She was also helping her friend with her wedding plans.

It would not be a lavish affair, but Tony knew too many important people who would be hurt not to be invited. A lot of them were curious about the woman who had captured their friend's heart. Therefore after the ceremony they planned a luncheon for fifty people. At least they did not have to get involved with a band and all the other trimmings associated with a reception. They had chosen a large hotel in downtown Chicago that had a banquet room on the top floor with awesome views of Lake Michigan. The banquet people would see to all the arrangements.

Phoebe also went out to dinner with them every Friday night. True to his word Tony made sure they went out with Hugh on Saturday night, so Phoebe did not have to be around him.

It was mid May when she finally realized that Hugh would be Tony's best man and she would have to be around him for the wedding. She had been trying so hard not to think about him. She had not given a thought to his being at the wedding. I guess I can survive the rehearsal dinner and a few hours on the wedding day she contemplated. I still have two weeks to prepare. I will just avoid him as much as possible.

Even after what he did to me, I still miss him. Maybe being back in Chicago reminds me of our time together. I had a lot of fun in Los Angeles with Abby, but there was an emptiness inside me. I don't know why I felt that way.

She had no plans to get involved with him or anyone. She would just have to work really hard to avoid him at the wedding. She did not want him to guess she still had feelings for him. The last thing she wanted was another relationship with him, so he could hurt her all over again.

It was about the same time that Hugh found out that Phoebe would be in the wedding, and that she had been in Chicago since early March.

"Why in the world didn't you tell me she was back here, Tony?"

"Because she specifically said she did not want to see you, and you intimated the same thing. She is helping at the camp this summer but she only agreed to do it, if you were not going to be there."

"I know I have been busy with a lot of other things relating to the camp and did not plan to spend my summer there. But I thought I would come for the 4th of July week and maybe for the last week."

"That's fine. She said, if you come up for a couple of weeks, she could live with that. She will be in charge of the children in the evening and will be staying in the cabin near the bunkhouses. You won't run into each other in the house. I think she plans to eat with the kids so they get to know her, so that also won't be a problem."

Hugh knew he had hurt Phoebe a lot when he broke up with her. After having time to think things through this last winter he realized it was the stupidest thing he had ever done in his life. But he did not know how to change things back. It was obvious she would go to whatever lengths she could to avoid him.

I almost had what Tony and Riley have, and I threw it away, he thought. I miss being around her. We always had so much fun together. No woman ever made me laugh the way she did, nor understood what I went through with Hillary.

I wish there was some way I could spend the rest of my life with her. But I don't think now there is any chance of that, more less getting her alone in the same room with me. Even if I did, she would probably not believe me, if I told her how I feel. Why should she? She would probably think I would just dump her again at some later time.

He thought about saying something to Tony, but decided against it. His friend was so happy and he did not want to bother him with his sadness. Especially since he did not believe it would do any good.

And so life continued as it was. Riley and Tony split their time between their two friends. They both wished things could go back to the way they used to be. The four of them had been so compatible and had such good times together. But it looked like that was not going to happen again.

Chapter 48

It was time for the wedding. Riley and Tony were so excited, and their happiness was contagious. Everyone enjoyed being around the couple. Phoebe realized she was uptight on the rehearsal evening with just the thought of seeing Hugh again.

However, things turned out better than expected. She and Riley drove up to the church at the same time as Tony and Hugh. As they exited their cars Hugh said, "Hello, Phoebe."

She nodded her head but then turned and went into the church with Riley without saying a single word to him. After that he made no attempts to talk to her. Since they stood on opposite sides of the church and at opposite sides of the dinner table, it was fairly easy to avoid each other.

Tony and Riley were concerned at first. But when nothing happened, they let their joy in each other take over and forgot their friends. The rehearsal dinner went smoothly. There was not a dry eye in the room when Tony took Riley's hand and said, "You have made me so happy, sweetheart. When you are unhappy in your marriage, it is like being in prison. Then suddenly it comes to an end, and you are free. You cannot help but feel a little guilty for feeling so happy. It is easy to be foolish and fall in love with someone who ends up making you unhappy. You have regrets and wish it never happened. But you, Riley, have made me realize that is no reason to close yourself off and shut out the world as I did."

Then he added, "Life is about having healthy relationships; not being codependent. It took me a long time to realize that. I kept ignoring what was going on with Ginger thinking it would get better. But we did not have a partnership. Instead I adapted to her moods. If she had a happy day, then so did I. If she was upset, I stayed away."

Riley reached up with her other hand and touched his face as he continued, "I did not understand that she behaved badly towards me, because deep inside she was afraid. I did not comprehend her anger was really fear, and it caused her to be very insensitive to my needs. She became very selfish. But I could not see that, because I was trying so hard to give her comfort and reassurance. Instead of trying to solve our issues we only alienated each other. By the time I realized what was happening, she was so immersed in her compulsive behavior there was no way to reach her."

As he looked at his friend briefly he continued. "But sometimes things happen due to luck. You and Hugh were dating casually. It would never have gone anywhere. But being friends with Hugh brought all four of us together for the train trip. Neither one of us was looking for a relationship. It seems odd how we teamed up together over the maps and driving when it should have been Hugh you bummed around with."

Hugh was glancing down at the table looking very sad as Tony finished. "Love happens to everyone but it does not seem ordinary when it happens to you. We read about all the young people falling in love but it can also happen to much older individuals who no longer believe it is possible. It brings joy and happiness and sometimes pain and sorrow. But it is definitely worth the effort to take a chance, and see where it leads. And I plan to spend as many years as we are given making you happy."

As she gazed at him, she knew she had found the man she had not known she was looking for. They would be together for the rest of their lives. Right now she had everything she wanted and needed.

Hugh did not look at Phoebe, but he had tears in his eyes. A pain shot through his heart at his friend's words. How could he have let her go? He and Phoebe could be as happy as their friends, if he had not been so afraid.

Since everyone was so delighted over the couple's happiness no one realized how sad Hugh was as he went out to the car after dinner.

Before they knew it the next day had arrived. The two women were in the side room at the church preparing for the wedding.

"I cannot believe how blissful I feel and how excited I am to be marrying Tony. I never thought I would feel this way again."

"I am so pleased for you Riley. You deserve every bit of happiness." Phoebe had told Riley what Abby had said about her friend and their years together. "I know the two of you will also have many wonderful years as a couple."

"I just wish you could, too, Phoebe. I am so contented. I wish you could be as happy as I am."

"Don't worry about me. I am very satisfied with my life. Come on. I hear the music. It is time for us to walk down that aisle."

As Phoebe walked down the aisle she started to look at Tony, but saw Hugh instead. He was staring at her with a strange look in his eyes. She felt a jolt of pain go through her and immediately lowered her eyes.

As they stood before the minister they heard him say, "Love can heal a dying soul. It may not make the world go round, but it makes the trip worthwhile. We only have one life to live. We should kiss slowly, forgive quickly, love truly, and laugh uncontrollably. Never regret anything that makes you smile. And never laugh at each other's dreams. People without dreams don't have much. Winter must be cold for those with no dreams or happy memories. I know you two will have many happy times together."

As they finished their vows Tony whispered to her, "I wish I had a time machine so I could relive this moment with you over and over."

What he said touched her deeply. As she glanced at him, he knew what that glance meant. After kissing her before God and the world he took her hand. They walked down the aisle as man and wife.

Today was the start of a brand new chapter in their lives. They were both looking forward to what would happen next with anticipation. Smiling at each other they got into the limo to go to their reception.

Chapter 49

The reception had been a lot of fun and Phoebe had managed to avoid Hugh. Now it was Monday morning and she was driving up to Minnesota on her own. She had packed everything she would need for the next two months. She would not use her car except for rare occasions. But she knew it was just as safe in Minnesota, as in her garage at home.

There was plenty of room in the barn for her to park. If she needed to make a trip to Duluth and the camp car was not available, she would not have to wait around for it to return. She knew she was being a little paranoid, but she would also have it there in case she had a problem when Hugh arrived. She could get away for awhile, if she needed to.

Phoebe had a neighbor who would take in her mail. The woman would send anything that seemed important up to the camp. She did not want to bother with having all her mail forwarded. Besides she never got anything very significant in the mail, since she did bill pay through her bank on the internet and had most of her bills sent by email.

Although she was a little sad when the familiar house

came into view, remembering the fun times she had with her friends last fall, she still had a sense of peace as if she was coming home. She knew she felt the way some of her friends did who had second homes. They had described their feelings when they returned after several months away.

Irene and Jerry had arrived about two hours before her and were busy opening the house and getting the water and heat turned on. Early June could still be cool, although it was not real cold and Irene wanted to take the chill out of the air.

Phoebe was staying on the second floor in one of the bedrooms. She did not want to go all the way up to the third floor. There was no need and she did not want to be reminded of the time she spent up there last year with her friends.

There were still over two weeks before the first week of camp would start. Adam had set up another committee, which Hugh chaired, that was making the lists of which children would attend and what week they would come. Meanwhile, next week the four teachers would arrive and begin their work of setting everything up for the water sports, games, crafts and activities.

Irene had spent the last two weeks before she arrived making lists of groceries she would need both in bulk and to feed everyone before camp started. She and Jerry had stopped in Moose Lake and picked up a few items including a broasted chicken so she would not have to cook that evening. The large chain store in Duluth was sending a truck the next day to deliver all the preordered groceries.

Phoebe had bought all the furniture for the bunkhouse

and her cabin a month previously. Everything had arrived at the furniture store. She planned to go to Duluth in the morning and check the inventory. She would also stop at the grocery store, if Irene needed anything else.

If everything was correct at the furniture store, two trucks would deliver all the items on Wednesday morning. There would be four men in the two trucks to set everything up. Once that was done the housekeeper from town who had been hired fulltime during the summer would help her clean and wipe everything down before making the beds.

Cupboards with doors had been built in beside each bed space. The children could put their clothes in the cupboards. Phoebe would also place a set of towels in each one. Besides towels each child would be assigned a beach towel for when they did any water activities. Towel racks had also been installed next to their beds. When they arrived, after unpacking, the kids would slide their empty suitcases under their beds.

The architect who had designed the bunkhouses had added double the original space to the prefab cabin. Phoebe would share a wall with the laundry room. Two large industrial strength washers and dryers had been placed in that room. Phoebe knew it would not bother her since washing would be done during the day when she would rarely be using her cabin.

Time seemed to speed by as all the preparations were coming together. Four high school girls from town had been hired to help Irene in the kitchen with the cooking and whatever else she needed. Two would work four days a week, and two would work three days. The days would be long with getting breakfast, lunch and dinner ready for so many people. Adam did not want to burn the girls out. Actually since it was only six weeks, the students were happy to have the work.

After the teachers got there life seemed to get very busy. Before everyone knew it the first week of camp had arrived. It was 1:30 a.m. when the bus rolled into the yard. Everyone had been resting, but they were ready to greet the first arrivals and get them settled.

It was after 2:00 a.m. by the time everyone was in bed. Breakfast and orientation was scheduled for 8:30 a.m. Many of the kids had slept a little on the bus. They also knew the children would be too excited to sleep too late in the morning.

At 8:00 a.m. Phoebe woke the camp counselors, and then went to the bunkhouses to get the girls and boys up. This first group that had come to camp was split equally with twelve girls and twelve boys. They were a little older. The committee knew they would need to work out some of the bugs through trial and error to see what worked and did not work for some of the activities. Therefore, they wanted kids who were older, knew how to swim, and could catch on to things a little quicker.

The older kids who were acting as camp counselors had been in training classes for two weeks prior to their arrival. They had even met with the four teachers a couple of times before they left to come to camp. Everyone knew this first week would definitely be a learning experience.

However Adam had chosen wisely. The four teachers were awesome. There were eight camp counselors, four boys and four girls, who had wanted to help for the summer.

And, they worked well with the teachers. Between the twelve of them and Phoebe, the kids had a wonderful time. Even Tony and Riley helped with some of the activities, especially the water sports and hiking. They also helped out in the house with whatever needed to be done.

When Saturday arrived it was a very sad time for everyone when the children had to leave. On Friday the housekeeper had washed the children's clothes. Saturday morning all the sheets and towels needed to be done. All the kids were taught to make their beds with help from the adults. That way the bunkhouses would be ready for the next incoming group. Camp counselors and staff would have their clothes and bedding washed on Monday mornings.

Everyone waved goodbye as the bus left right after dinner. When the sleeper arrived in Minneapolis the new kids would get on the bus and head to camp. The returning children would spend the night on the train before heading back to Chicago the next day when the Empire Builder arrived in Minneapolis.

A retired couple had been found who loved the idea of riding back and forth each week. The first week Riley and Tony had brought the children, but they wanted to stay the summer so they could not ride back and forth as they originally thought they would. One of Adam's staff rode up with everyone to make sure the sleeper went back to Chicago the next day. After the first weekend the retired couple would take over.

The next week was the 4th of July and when the children arrived Hugh and Adam were with them. Hugh was planning on staying on the second floor where the teachers were. He and Adam watched as everyone got the children settled into bed for the night.

Adam was extremely impressed with how organized everything went, and how awesome the whole camp looked. Although everyone worked hard, he knew he had Phoebe to thank for a lot of the work that had been done. He realized it had been a team effort. He was even pleased with himself that he had chosen such excellent teachers to run the day to day camp activities.

Thursday was the 4th of July and some special activities, as well as a cook out, had been planned. The camp was close enough to Moose Lake that the town's fireworks would be seen. This was a special week, Most of the children picked to come to camp were long term foster kids who had little or no hope of being placed. Adam hoped a couple of them might become camp counselors someday.

Phoebe had seen Hugh a few times and had politely spoken to him. But she had been so busy she had not been around him much. On Monday night she noticed her three friends and Adam sitting on the porch talking. It reminded her of all the times they had done that the previous fall.

She winced when she saw her friends on the porch, and was sad she was not sitting there with them. Adam, knowing how hard she had worked to make the camp a reality, had invited her to join them She was less distressed when she learned Adam wanted to include her. She was thinking of joining them. But she ended up having to decline when one of the kids cut his foot, and one of the counselors came to get her to help. By the time they had taken care of the boy and gotten him settled in bed she saw no one was sitting on the porch any longer.

Chapter 50

Hugh was upset with himself. He had done a lot of work to make this camp a reality and had been looking forward to spending the 4ᵗʰ of July up here. At the same time he was saddened to think that not only was Phoebe avoiding him, but she was not interacting with any of the other adults when he was around.

He realized now that he loved her. He did not want her to be hurt, because he had come up for the week. He knew Adam had invited her to sit on the porch with everyone. He thought she had declined, because he would be there. He did not know she was giving first aid to a little boy.

She had not seen him but he was still sitting on the porch when he saw her cabin light go on. He wanted to go over, knock on her door, and ask her to sit with him for a while. But he knew she would probably just slam the door in his face. And he even felt her action would be justified.

Now that Tony was settled into married life he had finally talked to his friend about his dilemma. Tony was happy to know how he felt about Phoebe. But like his friend, he was not sure what Phoebe's reaction would be, if he made an overture towards her. Both men thought she would not believe him.

Tony decided to talk to Riley to see if she had any suggestions on how Hugh could approach Phoebe. Neither one of them had much hope anything would help and they did not really blame her.

Meanwhile, the days passed quickly and the 4th of July arrived. The kids were having a wonderful time, and the cookout had gone well. A large bonfire had been built and everyone was looking forward to roasting marshmallows and making s'mores. It was getting dark. Tonight would be a late night due to the fireworks.

Hugh was sitting with Riley, Tony and Adam. When he looked around he no longer saw Phoebe sitting across from him where she had been. Deciding to walk down to the lake he got up quietly while everyone was singing camp songs.

As he walked to the pier, he saw Phoebe standing on it. A full moon was brightly shining and it seemed to light a path across the lake directly to her.

"Hi, Phoebe. Can I talk to you for a minute?"

"We don't really have much to say to each other," she answered him back sadly.

"I know I am the reason for that and I am truly sorry."

"It's okay Hugh. We have moved on."

Well maybe you have, but I haven't he thought to himself.

"I just wanted to tell you I am sorry about the other night."

"Sorry about what the other night?"

"I know Adam invited you to sit with us on the porch. I feel bad that you felt you had to avoid the others just because I was there."

"That is not why I did not come Hugh. I admit I am not comfortable being around you, but I could have sat on the other side of the porch. I had to give first aid to a little boy who cut his foot. That is why I was not there."

"Well, that is a relief."

When she looked at him strangely he said, "Sorry, I did not mean it was a relief he cut his foot. I meant it was a relief I was not spoiling your time by being here."

"Hugh, I know how hard you worked to make Adam's dream of having this camp become a reality. You have every right to visit whenever you want."

"I want you to know, Phoebe, I am very sorry I broke up with you. I was afraid of a long term commitment. I had a lot of time to think things through this winter and realized what a fool I was. I do not expect you to believe me, but I needed to at least tell you how I feel."

Before Phoebe could respond the sky lit up with the fireworks being set off in town. They could both hear all the oohs and aahs coming from the kids, as they stood their silently watching the sky.

When the fireworks ended Phoebe turned to say something to Hugh, but he was gone. That is strange she thought. I know I am uncomfortable around him but I never really thought it mattered to him one way or the other.

I do not want to upset him or have him think I am just trying to make him miserable for what he did to me. I knew going in he had problems with commitment. I just did not think I was putting any pressure on him. But something set him off last winter.

I guess I will never know what it was. Maybe I should try to be more pleasant to him from now on. It certainly will not hurt me to be nice to him. Having decided to change her course of action towards him, she walked off the pier and went to her cabin.

Chapter 51

The rest of the week flew by. Phoebe thought some more about what Hugh had said to her that evening on the pier. She realized he seemed very sad, whenever she saw him. But that did not mean she trusted him. Maybe now that Tony was married to Riley he just felt he needed a girlfriend. Although she had to admit he never had trouble attracting women previously.

She was not sure how she felt, but realized she was too busy to think about the situation for the present. However, Saturday night after the bus left for Minneapolis she went to rest up until it returned with the new batch of kids. She had smiled at him, and said goodbye when he and Adam left with the children.

As she waited for the incoming batch of new kids she thought once again about what he had said to her. Could he really have realized that he made a mistake breaking up with her? She was not sure what to think. They always had such fun times together and joked a lot.

There had been so many joyless years with Dan that it had felt good to laugh with someone again. And how about the way she had felt last winter? She had a good time with her family, but there was something missing she could not put her finger on. And they had a lot of values in common, especially the way they had both taken care of their spouses.

Maybe the next time he came up she should make a point to talk more to him. She was so ambivalent that when she had time a few days later she spoke to Riley about the situation.

"You are the one who has to make up your own mind, Phoebe. I know Hugh spoke to Tony and told him he loves you, but did not know how to tell you in a way you would believe him."

Phoebe's mouth dropped open when her friend told her about his declaration of love.

"Life is so short, Phoebe. As the minister said, we only have one life to live. He also said winter must be cold for those with no happy memories. I know you loved your husband, but you spent so many years dealing with his health issues there was no time for joy. Now we are in the winter of our lives. Like your friend Abby said all her happy memories make her life so much more worth living."

"I know you are right, Riley. I am not interested in marriage at this point, but I liked being with Hugh. However what happens if he breaks up with me again?"

"There are no guarantees. Sometimes you have to take a risk. But you are the one who must determine if being with him is worth the risk."

"I guess now I am even more confused than ever."

"That is not necessarily a bad thing, Phoebe."

Phoebe believed Hugh would be back one more time in July. She watched for him on Saturday nights when the bus arrived, but he was never on it. She had thought a lot about the situation and decided, the next time he came, she would talk to him.

Even if they just became friends again maybe that was enough. She wanted to see how he felt about that. Finally the last Saturday arrived with the last batch of kids. As they exited the bus she kept watching, but Hugh was not on it. She could not believe how disappointed she felt. Maybe they were destined to stay apart.

Monday afternoon she was helping to sort the counselors' clothes and sheets when she heard a car drive up. Who in the world can that be she wondered? As she looked out the laundry room window, she saw Hugh and Adam getting out of the car. Riley and Tony came out to greet the two men.

She left the laundry room and went to give Adam a hug while saying hello to Hugh.

"So what brought you two up here," she asked.

"You did not think we would leave all the work of closing this place down next week to just you. We came to help," Adam said.

"We can sure use it. Once these children leave on Saturday we will have a lot of work to do getting this place ready for winter."

"And that is exactly why we came," Adam said with a twinkle in his eyes.

The week past quickly. Soon it was Saturday afternoon. The kids were off with the teachers for a hike. As Phoebe came out of her cabin, she ran into Hugh.

She was a little taken aback, but quickly recovered. "Hi, Hugh. I guess now it is my turn to say I am sorry."

"You are sorry for what, Phoebe?"

"I did not want you to stay away from here all summer just because I was here."

"That is not why I stayed away," he said as they walked down to the lake together.

"Good. I am glad it was not me."

"Actually I have been working with Adam on setting up a tax free entity here. We plan to have a yearly auction to help fund things. We were making plans for that. Adam wants to add two more weeks to camp next year. He is thinking of adding horses and all his ideas will add to the cost of running the place. It seems like we have had meetings with his financial advisors all summer and time just slipped away."

"I don't know how to tell you this, but I have been thinking about our talk that night on the pier. I wanted to say something to you, but when I turned you were gone."

"Does that mean you don't hate me anymore?"

"I never hated you, Hugh. You hurt me and being around you was very painful."

He winced when she said that. He reached out and

took her hands and said, "I told you I had a lot of time to think about us last winter. She stared at him as he gazed into her eyes. I know you probably will not believe me but your life means more to me than anything. I love you. I feel differently now. I do not feel unsure about things anymore. I have lived alone for so long, but since I left you I am lonely. I do not want to end up a bitter old man, because I did not seize the opportunity for love when it was being given to me."

He then continued, "When I saw you again over the 4th of July my heart skipped a beat. I realized how bleak and empty my life has been since I lost you. Love burns in my heart for you. There is no one else I want to be with. I want you to be my wife and lover and best friend."

As she started to say something he said, "Let me finish. Jealousy and manipulation are not aspects of love. I can clearly see that is what I had with Hillary. I kept thinking I could make things better and help make her better. But that was wrong. Only she had the capacity to make herself better. For some reason she chose not to. She put such guilt on me and I accepted it. A lot of what Tony said that evening of the rehearsal dinner got through to me."

She had tears in her eyes as he continued. "I wish I had done something about my marriage years ago. After you left I knew I needed help to come to grips with things. So I went to the psychologist you and Riley saw. I did not even tell Tony. The doctor helped me to see things from a different perspective. I was finally ready to accept what he was saying. I kept thinking the same problems would somehow happen all over again to us. But I realized you and I are not Hillary and me. When I accepted that I understood what a tragedy had occurred when I lost you."

As he tilted her chin up towards him, he saw the tears in her eyes. He could not stand it any longer. He gathered her up in his arms. He buried his face in her hair, and as his voice cracked he said, "I love you. Leaving you hurt so bad." He was holding her so tight it almost hurt. But she did not mind. She needed the comfort and warmth of his embrace. She wrapped her arms more tightly around his neck.

As she looked at him with adoring eyes and a glow on her face she was trembling, and it stunned her. He made her ache and she now knew he felt the same about her. Her skin was hot, and she heard the thud of his heart. "Hugh," she murmured, "We have the rest of our lives to be together."

Looking at her with a yearning that surprised him, their lips met and passion exploded.

Epilogue

It was September, and the camp had been closed for two weeks. Things were progressing for the auction and camp plans for the following year. The two couples were at Union Station ready to board the Pullman. This time they would take the Empire Builder west. Once they got past Minneapolis all the sights would be new.

They were so excited to be able to visit Glacier again. They just hoped they would not get caught in snow this time. It was starting to be late in the season for the park.

Hugh was still trying to talk Phoebe into marrying him. But she liked just getting to know him all over again. Maybe at some point they would marry, but for now she was happy with things as they were.

Hugh had agreed to spend the winter in California getting to know her family. Leaving the Chicago winters behind, while being with Phoebe was appealing to him. When Riley and Tony heard their plans they wanted to go with them. Abby had found two condos in her building on the same floor that were being rented out for the winter.

Both couples signed leases which started the first of

November. They planned to drive out to California, so they would have a vehicle. But for now, they had their new train trip to look forward to.

After the Empire Builder they would take the Coast Starlight down to Los Angeles where they planned to spend a few days meeting Phoebe's family. Then they would ride the Southwest Chief back to Chicago.

They heard the announcement for First Class passengers to board. They walked out to the platform where Margaret and Charles were waiting for them with big smiles. As they climbed the steps of the Pullman, they heard Charles say, "All Aboard."